How Fatima Started Islam

Mohammad's Daughter Tells It All

NOOR BARACK

Printed in the United States of America

ISBN: 978-0-578-03290-0

Dedication

This book is dedicated to all the American and the world wide coalition of military personnel stationed in the Middle East. This book is especially dedicated to those members who heroically made the supreme sacrifice to keep the world safe from radical and terroristic islam.

Foreword

The shrouds of history obscure, alter, and color the ancient events; while competing interest have always attempted to mold history to benefit their individual causes. When events happen among non-literate people, the distortions, deceptions, and outright lies quickly overtake the truth. After absolutism and fanaticism are added to the mix with illiteracy, the modern world receives a story that cannot possibly be accurate.

In addition to the above problems, within the Islamic community are various traditions, which are saturated with mistrust, fear, and hatred for each other, and espouse radically different interpretations of important founding principles and facts.

From the seventh century to the twenty-first internecine disputes between the different Islamic factions have resulted in millions of deaths. Even today, in the early twenty-first century, it is still a DAILY occurrence of one Muslim killing another Muslim over what is taught, worshipped or believed. The fact of daily intra-Muslim slaughter is ridiculous to all except those directly involved. Both sides cannot each be totally right. But, the radicals and terrorists on all sides will defend their versions of the revealed truth by bringing death to those not into complete agreement. This absurdity should be apparent to any thinking person.

What really happened in Arabia in the seventh century is unknowable. There are many people who claim that they know exactly what happened and will gladly kill any infidel who disagrees. But any true student of history knows that fifty generations is way too far back, especially in a culture largely illiterate with no freedom of thought or disagreement.

So knowing that the murky, nebulous beginnings of Islam are unknowable, and that the present traditions are almost certainly false; I have devised my own made-up history of that period. I do not claim it to be truth, just another possible scenario on the enigma of early Islam. Knowing, to some extent, how humans operate, I believe my little fantasy is probably as accurate as orthodox Islam is in its various, and mutually opposed traditions. It is up to the reader to assign whatever degree of belief the reader wishes to, including no belief whatever.

It is my political opinion that these forays into what some people consider sacred, is good. Thought held by militant orthodoxy, that their ideas are unchallengeable is destructive to truth and world brotherhood. It is anathema to a stable world when people are afraid of offending extremists who claim that their dogma is the only legitimate one and that they can trash all competing ideas, but all others must kowtow to their ideas because only their ideas are sacred and sacrosanct.

In short, I have broadly tried to humorously poke fun at some people who are not known for being fun loving, and to make less serious the tenets of a belief. I believe we have to fearlessly show that all faiths, people, cultures, religions, and ideas are on an equal footing in the market place of human endeavor, and that no one person or group is above anyone else. I believe that this is actually how to better understand one another and that bridge building is achieved by democratizing all beliefs. We cannot attain the goal of just getting along, if groups cling to a superior attitude because they believe that only they have the truth. In an odd way, things like this little book will eventually help achieve mutual understanding and respect when people can look at themselves and others on an equal footing.

I shall close by saying that the history of the world is pointed in certain directions. These directions make me very happy even though we have a long way to go. Worldwide individuals are gaining and have gained more control over their fate. People are allowed to think, express, and believe much more than ever before. These individual rights have been expanded to minorities, gays, women, handicapped, and even hated people. We can go back in our debt of gratitude to ancient Athens and its modern equivalent of the West. We have not achieved universal freedom, but it should be coming. I live in the United States. I have seen the blessings of a free press and media, the total freedom of religion, the individual rights of free assembly and speech. I have seen humanity flourish because no tyrant, prince, or religion can block discussion of any topic or viewpoint. It is to this ideal that the world should strive and which engendered my profane little fantasy.

CHAPTER 1

In the Beginning

I have to set the record straight. Not that you can expect total accuracy after 1400 or so years, but this thing has become so totally distorted that the true facts just have to come out.

Allow me introduce myself; my name is Fatima, daughter of Mohammad and granddaughter of Abdullah. I was born about 14 centuries ago and I was both blessed and cursed with my birth. I was blessed with extremely high intelligence, great physical beauty, and a pleasant disposition. I was cursed by being born a girl into a family of drunken, imbecilic pimps in the dirty, smelly, illiterate hellhole of the hamlet of Mecca, within the barren, ugly, oppressively hot region called Arabia. Or, as we who live here like to say, the land of sand, morons, and camelshit. Needless to say, things did not look bright the day I was dropped into this world.

This was not only before electricity and running water, but practically before food. I mean we were only about three generations from sharing caves with wild jackals.

Primitive. . . . people still talked with awe over the discovery of fire.

Fortunately, a few good things did happen to me soon after my birth. My intelligence was too great not to be noticed even by my dull and drunken family. No one seemed to care that much, but perhaps a little flame was lit, so that just maybe my gifts could become useful. My beauty was recognized early and they certainly did care about that. As a small child I sought out different people who spoke other languages and was fascinated by the various tongues, and with a child's inborn grasp of language learning, I was soon conversing in the related Hebrew, Egyptian, vulgate and other speech families.

Our tribal compound, which was near the middle of town, was in constant motion since the family dealt in provisions, slaves, camel trading and the mainstay of our business, a combination saloon and brothel. I was reared in the middle of the largest activity center in this backwater, hayseed center of nothingness.

At the age of four Ra'hel was brought into my life. She was a slave brought in on one of the caravans and traded for two exclusive evenings with Adelphi, who was our most beautiful and expensive 'working girl' in the brothel. Although Ra'hel was very old, almost 50, she had a regal charm and dignity not befitting that of a slave. She had obviously not been born to slavery or brought up in it and was totally quiet about the misfortunes of life that had landed her here at this forgotten, dirty corner of the world. I always thought that I must have reminded her of someone associated with better times, perhaps a daughter or granddaughter, because she was the first person who ever showed me kindness and love.

Ra'hel asked permission to teach me reading and numbers and the request was granted, since having someone in the family who could read might come in handy. Girls in Arabia were generally allowed to do nothing-they were to be sold, bear children, work and clean. But my family was always looking for new ways to make money in any way they could and welcomed anything that might have a profit attached to it. She also taught me Farsi the language of her birth. She never explained how she had been favored with letters and numbers, but she understood and taught me the different writing systems needed for the different languages as well as both regular and the hard to manipulate Roman numbers.

I loved having my mind expanded. The problem was that as I gained more knowledge and understanding, the gross stupidity of everybody else in this town became sickeningly apparent. I was determined, by the age of eight, to rise above this flyblown life of degradation, dirt and stupidity, whatever it took, wherever it took me, and no matter what sacrifices I had to endure. I was not, barring an early death, going to live the life my family had planned for me, if anyone, in fact, had ever bothered to give my future a single thought.

By that age of eight, Ra'hel and I were keeping the

accounts and I could gauge that a lot of shekels were coming in, but, and this was no surprise, most of it was being squandered. We were making our archrival Dhinnah family very wealthy by our labor, because they controlled the liquor transportation monopoly, and used their position to squeeze our profits dry. I also met at age eight my mother's mother and I could not believe that this intelligent refined lady had produced the drunken slut who, in turn, produced me. Grandma was not happy with the house, her daughter, her son-in-law, the business or anything else in Mecca besides me. I now knew two strong women I could look up to and it helped me realize that not every female was a lowlife addicted chippy.

My grandmother was around for a little less than a complete month, but what a month that was, full of inspiration, admiration and hope. I knew she talked to my parents about me, and my potential, but it was futile and it failed to change anything, sadly within two years she had died back in Aden where she and my mother hailed from. But I was so glad that I had finally met my grandmother and had learned that not everyone in my family was so creepy, slovenly, stupid, and drunk. It gave me more hope and evidence that I was not destined to continue this ugly, dirty, undignified life that I was born into.

By age eleven I had begun to show slight signs of physical adolescence, and with my childhood ending, it was my turn to enter the family business.

CHAPTER TWO

My Monumental Year

The year that started just before I turned twelve was the absolute biggest year of my life. Far more happened to me during that year than in all the other years combined. I may have been smart, but as a young girl in Arabia I had ZERO say over my circumstances. This would change, but I had to follow my three elder sisters (dumb, dumber, and Oh my god I know two camels that are smarter) into the family business.

So on the eve of my twelfth birthday, with little fanfare and very matter-of-factly, I was turned out as a whore. The family compound offered little privacy, hygiene, or respect, so observing random sexual acts was a daily delight. The slave whores, the free whores, and my sisters before their retirement and marriages were all on the, shall we say, immodest side. The local yokels and camel jockeys who were the bulk of the customers generally would screw one of these chippies anywhere and everywhere. A few of the more elderly town fathers demanded some privacy, but the whole compound was a visual sea of sexual perversions. I mean we could have charged admission into this freak show.

Knowing what was in store for me years before the actuality meant that I did observe and in a sense prepare myself. It was just a fact of life. There was no sense crying about it because I had known for years that this was going to be my adolescent fate. What did bother me was how I was going to be initiated.

I did discuss at length with Ra'hel the events, which the family insisted on calling my "first nuptials". She was horrified about the coming virtual enslavement and sacrilege but did her best to comfort me, hide her horror, and gave me practical advice on trying to maintain my dignity, equanimity, and sanity.

The plan was that I would follow the pathways of my older sisters which consisted of putting in about five years under the filthy camel jockeys, retire from the profession, spend a year being cleansed and revirginated, and then finally being married off to probably some drunk who knew my father. Even at eleven I realized that this had 'sick' written all over it, but this was the family into which I had the misfortune to be born. As a matter of practicality some of the customers liked fresh, young meat and I was that year's baby whore.

So I had to be broken in and put to work. Now even at eleven, I knew how this should be done in a profitable way. Sell or auction the young virgin to one of the wealthy men and make some good money, but not in Mohammad's household. Disgusting and perverted as it was, the old sot had to break in every new girl personally, including us his daughters. Now it was important to him and he even drank a little less on my 'joyous marriage night', but he was getting more decrepit and less potent so an experienced old hand accompanied us to our mat to act as a fluff girl to help delimp the ancient whoremaster. You can imagine my virginal bliss at being pawed, drooled on, and entered by this flatulent, filthy, camel breathed man who was my dad. Even though I treasure the memory, I think I would have preferred being gang raped by a troop of chimpanzees, and it would have felt more normal. My thoughts of escape from this perverted bedlam got a gigantic boost that magical night

I received two days and one night off to recover and then I was on the block, and also on the floor, and on the grass, and on the dirt. I had to screw guys everywhere but the top of a camel. There were no psychiatrists in Mecca at the time but I could have used about a dozen and the household could have used about 100.

Now I hate to admit this, but I have decided to quash all the lies, mistakes, and fabrications, even if it is personally embarrassing, but I actually did like a few of the younger, good-looking guys. After screwing all these old guys, sweaty Nubians, fat slobs, drunken morons, and certified lunatics; a clean young manchild with a good body and hungry appreciative sparkle in his eyes, looked pretty good to me. Now that was how to make money, screwing a guy who you actually wanted to screw. It did not happen all that often, but thank Allah it did happen.

Adding to my general and day-to-day misery, this was when my best friend, my mentor, my 'true' mother Ra'hel got sick and quietly passed away. I blamed and still blame my family. What was happening to me bothered and embittered her tremendously, she even felt more disgust and revilement than I did. I was being hardened quickly and her gentle rose, her rainbow child, as she liked to call me, was becoming jade – beautiful but cold and unfeeling. I believe she took it to heart and her one joy in this ugly place, her one blooming radiant flower among the rocks and thorns was being degraded, coarsened, and sullied. Perhaps she was thinking of the girl I had reminded her of, and the probable fate of that unlucky flower. Suddenly she quickly sickened and died, and I am sure she did not want to live and see any more of this world.

I was inconsolable. Never had I felt such grief. It was at that dark point, surrounded by the void and vacuum of nothingness, within the empty, naked, frozen wasteland within the pith of my formless soul, that the revelation came to me loud and clear. Out of my misery and sorrow burst forth insightfully the eternal, ageless truth, that there is no God.

And, the all encompassing irony of ironies happened to me that fateful year, the largest irony of all human history. The biggest joke ever played on the story of humankind, the year that I saw the light to the fact that this world is godless, the over powering majestic revealed truth, that there is no God, never has been a God, and never will be a God, that was the year history changed, for that fateful year was the year when I founded the religion of Islam.

CHAPTER THREE

The Beginning of Islam

It was the convergence of four separate events that allowed me to amalgamate this quartet of circumstances into the new, and very powerful, monotheistic religion. Although it was founded by me, orchestrated by me, controlled by me, and nursed into existence by me, I could never publicly take control or credit. Being a woman, and even better a twelve-year-old whore, I could never be proclaimed as the instigator. Later on, after the religion became all-powerful, and took on a life of its own, the biographies of the principals could be sanitized to the point of ridiculousness. I would be elevated to an exalted, wise mother figure in a mutually loving, respectful relationship with my messianic father. Talk about putting lipstick on a she-camel.

But when you control the lives of the people, when you have life and death power over everyone, then the camelshit becomes tradition, and the tradition becomes fact, and the fact becomes the revealed truth of Allah. At the point of a sword, who will not swear undying loyalty to the sword wielder? The few who do refuse will accomplish nothing except that they will set a good posthumous example to the others. It actually took a few hundred years to completely whitewash all the blemishes, but death and the creditable threat of death has a way of quelling ugly rumors, whether they be true or not.

So when happenstance visited me with the perfect timing of events and circumstances I was ready to seize the moment and race with the camel. I could not publicly name the four founding principals that allowed the religion to start and flourish, but within my mind I revered what I called the four pillars of Islam.

The first pillar of Islam, in a sense the key to the very beginning of the religion, is the camel. It was actually one specific camel named Old Mama, but she was a representation of all the camels needed for the rapid, bloody spread of Islam.

For those fortunate enough to have no personal knowledge of the beasts let me give some brief background. Camels are large, ugly animals who were genetically engineered for deserts. They have a tough skin that smells really bad, an evil, foul breath that can kill small animals and children, a stubborn nature that a mule could envy, and all this is coupled with a colossal stupidity. In short, the camel is a metaphor for the land of Arabia. Among the locals there is a constant argument on whether the camel was made for Arabia or Arabia made for the camel.

But many of our men, and even some women, seem to love these flatulent stinkpots. When the wind is right a caravan, and even sometimes a single camel, can be smelled before it can be seen. Needless to say, those associated with the animals retain an unfortunate aura of camelness about their person. Add this to the general lack of rain and water of the region and you have many persons seriously questioning why people were born with noses. The vast majority of the population never gets totally used to it: and pity the few who do, and become walking plagues of stink. My father Mohammad seemed to relish in camelstink. It added one more assault upon me on my night that I was raped into womanhood.

Now like many camelmen, the old sot had a favorite camel, which was his bimmy. A bimmy was a pet camel that shared a special relationship with her master. Old Mama was Mohammad's bimmy for many years and he seemed to love this obstinate, moody, and gaggingly foul smelling animal. The main reason for the affection was that Old Mama when commanded would lower and angle herself whenever Mohammad wanted to fuck her. As he got older his sexual liaisons with the beast lessened and she did die before he did. But he was famous for getting blind drunk and humping Old Mama in every public place in Mecca. The citizens of Mecca do not have high standards for anything, but even among that crowd his drunken behavior with Old Mama was considered bush league and a cause of public derision as well as constant off color jokes.

The way Islam was actually started was like this. One night as I was approaching thirteen, and in total unhappiness with my horrible life, my father was out and about and got into his usual state of stupor. For whatever reason he decided to come home and sleep it off at the complex. He managed to get on Old Mama with no problem and she put it into automatic and headed toward home as she had done a thousand times before. When the pathway diverged into a fork with one branch going left and other right, Old Mama headed right the way to our quarters. Dear old dad in his fog was confused and sure that the way to go was left. He steers Old Mama to the left but she still wanted to go right. He got pissed, both literarily and figuratively, and started kicking and hitting her with a stick. Old Mama angrily stopped and purposely bucked with Mohammad being thrown off. This had all happened before and was no big deal, but this time he landed head first on a rock. He lay there for about fifteen minutes before he was discovered and carried back to the complex unconscious.

He lay like that until the middle of the second day when he awoke, his body had detoxed all the booze, he ate some food, talked normally and went immediately back into a state of unconsciousness for another 24 hours. Mohammad again awoke, ate heartily and communicated quite normally. About five hours later he went into a trancelike state and began to talk in total gibberish. This was absolutely unlike his drunken slurred and nearly impossible to comprehend ramblings, which we were all used to, but a sober sounding, even authoritative clear speech of absolute nonsense.

He went in and out of this trancelike state. Of course, when he was appearing normal, he was asked about the odd behavior and speech. He stated that he had no idea he was doing anything and no memory of acting at all unusually. He was a little scared and he kept to himself more and drank less. The alcohol did not seem to affect the weird gibberish states one way or the other.

So, after another few days, things were pretty normal as I am still keeping the cash accounts and screwing every horny moron who could beg, borrow, or steal two shekels. I had briefly talked to my father about raising the rates in the brothel because I was very sure that we would make more money, also at the same time we would have slightly less volume with me off my back a little more. I figured that if we raised the rates 50% we would only lose about 10% of the tricks for an increased profit of 35%. Naturally he dismissed the idea off hand.

After the evening meal break, when only the slave whores were available, I decided that the time was approaching. Mohammad was slurping over a roasted camel neck when he went into the trance and started babbling incomprehensible foolishness in a deliberative way. It was as if he were expounding on an important point in an intelligent way if you did not know him and know that the syllables coming out were pure nonsense. It was the third time that day that he had began to speak gibberish so the awe and wonder had faded a little bit.

I rose and went right next to him. Everyone was looking

at me and all was quiet as I waited a few seconds and then announced, "I can understand what he is saying."

CHAPTER FOUR

Mohammad Speaks

My mother, always a hearty eater, put her broiled camel's heart down an asked, "What is he saying?"

I had planned my actions and made the pronouncement, "He is saying that the price of pussy must go up." And I repeated "he keeps on saying it in different ways 'The price of pussy must go up- for every shekel it is now a shekel and one half.'"

All the eyes at the table just stared at me. I repeated myself again "He just keeps on saying the same things in different ways, that the brothel fees are too low and are to be immediately raised."

Around this moment he began to slow his speech and his steady, deliberate manner left him to his usual slovenly demeanor. I approached him and said, "Father, you were talking again and I was able to understand you as you wisely gave orders."

"What did I say?" as he looked astonished with bug eyes.

"You ordered that the price of pussy must go up

– immediately, for every old shekel the tricks must now pay a shekel and a half."

At this point a lot was riding on his reaction. I thought that it would go the way that it did go, but I was very apprehensive until it happened. He looked at the full table of people, his retinue of family and supporters and hangers-on. He was, after all, the boss of this little speck of Mecca.

He mustered what little dignity he could and declared, "I have been thinking about this for a long time, but tonight is the perfect time to put my ideas into place. As of this moment, henceforth and for all time, at Mohammad's Saloon & Brothel, the rates for pussy have just risen. Fatima, figure out how much it is for each chippy and tell them the new price."

I demurely acknowledged his command and left the table to begin the rounds of telling all the girls the new rates. I left the room violently suppressing my inward joy.

Yes, there was some small grumbling when the customers were informed, but that is what drunks do, they grumble. They do not change their actions at all, they just grumble.

While all this was going on, waiting for me in the grog shop having a couple of mugs, were the twins. The twins were very regular customers of mine who were outwardly as identical as two sand dunes in the desert. They often played a game they liked and would impersonate each other and were almost never caught because of the exactness that they owned. I relished in the fact that they could not fool me because they screwed so completely differently.

I had the extreme pleasure of informing them; that I was now a three shekel whore, and that every other girl in the place was also more money. They looked, as if, I had taken a knife and started stabbing their camel's thighs, they were so down trodden.

"But nobody will come." Said the first not realizing the double meaning.

"That may be true, but if you want some action from me it is three shekels a piece." I purposely rejoined, and wiggled a little for emphasis.

They were young and it did not take much to get them stimulated, "Well it's too far to go anywhere else, so okay for tonight, but this will be the last time."

"Up to you" I said as I took the older twin to my mat and give him the usual great screw. His younger brother then came in and then a few more.

When I reported to my father the next morning how much more money we had made and how smart it was for him to have raised the rates he was very pleased. He said maybe we should double it again and make even more money. I explained to him that he did not say this while in his 'wise trance' so it might not be a good idea. He reflected and agreed with me. He asked me if I thought that he would be saying many more wise things in the future. I assured him that he would. He seemed very happy as he headed to the grog room.

If only he knew how many wise things he would be saying.

It was with this first interpreted gibberish, those magical initial words, "The price of pussy must go up.", that the holy book of books, the revealed word of Allah, the book known as the Koran was born.

CHAPTER FIVE

The Koran Speaks

I had so many ideas and so much to do, but I had to be careful to not rush anything and thereby blow the whole setup. At the time Arabia was mostly polytheistic with lots and lots of gods. Whatever was inexplicable or even hard to understand was one more reason to have another god. Why does it sometimes rain, because of the rain god. Why do fish live in the sea? The fish god put them there. With this group of illiterates there were hundreds of hard to understand things, hence there were hundreds of gods.

Now there were Jews and their cousins the Christians around and it seemed that going with one god was better to me because it was easier to control things. The way it worked, when I was a child, was that the different devotees were always bickering, or worse, with each other over which god was more powerful. The sun god group was unhappy with the camel god group and they were each unhappy with the palm tree god group. It would be hard to get unity with the different factions, so I came up with the monotheistic plan, "There is but one god."

Before I could start with that mantra I had to rehabilitate

the old sot. I left word with everybody that I was to be called, even if I was 'engaged' with a trick, if Mohammad was babbling incoherently. He seemed to be in the state about two to three times a day. I informed everyone, including my father, that he was saying that he had been talking to god. When I was asked which god I said that I did not know, that Mohammad just said god. I did not ask him what he was saying I only reported what was theoretically said.

The news caused some stir within the dusty streets of Mecca because nothing like this had ever happened before. I also privately talked with my father and told him that what I was about to say were for his ears only. I told him I had a message from the 'wise figure' to the man Mohammad. The message was that he should drink less, cavort less, and take better care of his looks and bearings because he was going to be a very important man in charge of great things. My father seemed astonished but readily agreed to try. This was the part that was the real struggle, he did try, but you could only hope for so much from an ignorant, alcoholic, openly flatulent old camel jockey.

I wanted him to be more sane and sober for several reasons and the most important was that he had to live for at least a few more years, and with his lifestyle he was very liable to all types of diseases and accidents.

So I took some time to formulate my plans and we were making more money, and I was getting more control over the cash flow. Not only was the money coming in more rapidly, but I was noticing that the outgo was less. We paid the free girls one shekel out of four and the slave girls got one shekel out of ten to encourage good working habits and to give a long-term hope of buying their freedom. This was largely illusionary and pie in the sky, but it had happened that a few were able to become free in this way. A few others had their slavery brought by rich customers and some of them freed by their new masters. So with the percentage staying the same, the girls were getting more money, but that did not explain why there was more money than there should have been at the end of every week.

Then the revelation hit me, the reason we were doing so well was that with me watching the cash flow so closely there was much less chance of theft. With a drunken Mohammad in charge the family was being robbed blind. With me more or less taking over, it was much harder to get away with anything and the thief risked losing his hands, balls, or head. Anybody who stole from me was going to pay the price and I think that message got out there quickly, loudly, and clearly without being directly said.

I tried to observe who seemed real unhappy or resentful to me in order to identify the thieves, since I was sure there had been several who had become our 'partners'. I decided to let it all go because under the old Mohammad way, it was so easy to take advantage that anyone with an ounce of brains and a little courage would be a fool not to steal. With the new system of having the fool out of the picture, I might be able to use the more ambitious members of the household.

So the first immediate goals were to garner some respect for the village idiot and also to increase the cash flow. I began reporting that Mohammad was saying some wise, even profound, things. This was important for a couple of reasons. The first to show that he was not what everybody thought, but also to show that the obvious change was a miraculous change, inspired by a godlike patron.

He began to talk about how Arabia was great with a wonderful past and an even greater future. He forcefully spoke about how the blood feuds must stop if Mecca and Arabia were to enter the realm of greatness. The next step was that he commanded that both sides of some of the well-known family, and intra family disputes must come to him for settlement with all parties agreeing in advance to follow his dictates. No one seemed to catch on that what he was saying was unconnected random gibberish non-sense, which no one in the world could possibly make any sense of, and that I, a young girl who was for sale to any filthy camelboy or drunk for three shekels was calling the shots. Girls had no value except to take care of men and the thought of an educated, insightful one was too fantas-tic to even imagine.

In a matter of weeks he was, through me, settling dis-putes with intelligence, justice, and compromise and building up his power and prestige, which was growing within the municipality. The time had come to take the next step.

CHAPTER SIX

A Whore No More

Although I was in the radiant bloom of youthful adolescence, just chock full of exuberant energy, I was wearing myself out. Even while I was oraling a fat Nubian or being pounded by a middle-aged caravan leader, I was often in deep thought about my plans.

One evening, when the twins came in, my course of action had become clear. They were my most regular customers and whenever they had the urge it was a fast six shekels, and being healthy and having a rich father they often felt the desire. This is what happened that wonderful night about two and one half months after Old Mama had put into action the entire shebang. I was doing my usual first screw with the oldest as the younger watched. This visual foreplay always seemed to turn him on as his brother got first dibs, or maybe fourteenth dibs if you started the count at the beginning of the day. I was happy because it meant less time for me in the saddle. I could not have cared how these guys got excited as long as they more quickly shot their wads and got off my belly. So the oldest is getting close when a servant comes to me while

I am engaged and says, " Your father is talking in his new strange way again."

I did not want to lose the three shekels or have to later start over, so I acknowledged that I had gotten the message and used my experience as to how to enflame men sexually and got him to almost immediately climax. I put myself together and ran to listen to old camel breath rattle on his babble, leaving the younger one in an unsatisfied state.

When dearest dad finally stopped and regained his marginal sanity, I reported to him what he had said. What I told him was that he had said that I, Fatima, daughter of Mohammad, granddaughter of Abdullah, was to immediately begin being revirginated. I had turned my last trick and would regain my purity, unless for some unknown reason I wanted to be lovingly held by a good-looking manboy of my own choosing. I would be a whore no more.

Enough time had passed and this was after all an order, and not only that it was an order from Allah. I went back to the twins and explained that I had retired and brought along a new, and very attractive slave girl who was just slightly older than I was. I told the younger brother that because of his disappointment of not being able to possess me, I would substitute the new girl, at no charge; but I still needed three shekels from his older brother. I put those shekels away so I would be able to remind myself, when I became extremely rich and powerful, how far this baby chippy had come.

The younger one was not all that happy, but I had retired and he certainly was not going to turn down an attractive freebie.

So I would now have the time to stop going after the chump change, and use my real skills and time much more productively.

I had recently attained the age of thirteen and I was perhaps the youngest girl ever to successfully retire from whoredom. From now on all my orifices were entirely mine, and it would continue that way even if Mohammad received a divine revelation that I was to marry a man I would choose. I needed more time because the town's astonishment was beginning to fade and jealousy and opposition to our greater wealth and power was beginning to foment.

CHAPTER SEVEN

Jockeying for Power

The way Mecca operated when I was a child, and this was true in just about all of Arabia, was that the leading families were always in disputes and bickering with one another. This would be interspersed with chaos when subject to outside attacks or when the feuds broke into open homicidal warfare. When attacked from the outside, the town could, very temporarily, more or less cooperate in the defense until the immediate threat would lessen and then the bickering and jockeying would quickly resurface.

The feuds and intrigues were often along bloodlines, wherein all the families were connected by blood and marriage and it seemed that the closer the relationships were, the higher level of mistrust and jealousy. The main group that we had to worry about and watch: and who would be automatically opposed to us, were our cousins and constant rivals the Dhinnah clan.

Because of the horrible climate, no alcohol was actually manufactured in Mecca but was all brought in from the outside. It was easier to bring in the product, than to import all the ingredients needed and then make the booze. The Dhinnahs guarded their monopoly to the point of murder. Anyone could bring in their own booze for the household's use, but to bring in commercial quantities would invite death. They had their own saloon & brothel and would use their monopoly to gain advantage from all the other saloon keepers.

Fortunately for us the old head of the family Yusef died and his son known at Fat Yusef had taken over. The father was a tough adversary while the son was another drunken moron for which the region is famous. Fat Yusef had screwed me several times and although he was not yet 30 years old he was soft, as well as, ignorant, and treacherous. His only good trait was that he would somewhat regularly bathe. He came over maybe five or six times a month to drink and whore around, but it was partially to spy on how well we were doing.

My first, outside of the family actions, would be to neutralize these dangerous relatives and the other powerful families of Mecca. We certainly wanted Fat Yusef to continue in control because his younger brothers were at least a little smarter and a pack of vicious thugs into fighting and murder. Our compound would not be surprised if Fat Yusef met an untimely death at the hands of one of his younger brothers.

I decided that we should set up a small defense tax, which Mohammad would allegedly control. It had to be very minor, but the symbolism was important. Like all taxes if could be replaced by a larger tax later.

I had set it up so, that when old camelfart went into his gibberish, he was to be taken to a room away from the main activities, where I could be there alone with him. I then could interpret his jabber without distractions or witnesses. It was living hell being with this crazed idiot spouting off his nonsense but it had to be done. I made sure that absolutely no one was to be hovering around or to dare interrupt us.

Mohammad came down with a pronouncement that Mecca was in danger of attack and that we would all be much safer if we would be smart and take precautions. The precautions were that a little money would be assigned to each powerful family and a small constabulary raised which would supplement our defenses when trouble came, and that trouble was coming.

We would control the money, hire the outside guards and station them next door to our compound, which meant that they would be buying their booze and girls from us.

There was resistance but about 70% of the families complied out of fear or duty. We recruited some mean looking, tough, thugs from the coast and billeted them next door with a leader and sub leader. They were to be ostensibly out of any intra-Meccan affairs, but they were really the start of a private army. I delivered a secret message to the lieutenant in charge that Mohammad had stated that god had commanded that within three weeks the lieutenant was to figure out which recruit was the worst for whatever reason and to find an excuse to execute this recruit in front of the small company. I had decided that discipline was paramount if we were to go forward, by slaughtering one goat the other goats would get the message.

We were spending more money on the guards than was coming in from the tax, but that was all right since that situation would not last for too long. At the end of the first month the recruits, less one, were ready to be tested.

Out of the families who refused to pay the small defense tax, the Dhinnahs were the most powerful. If they gave in the others would follow. I could not see it, and I only got the report second hand, but this is what happened. The company of guards and some of our men went over to the Dhinnah saloon & brothel and the lieutenant demanded the tax for the upcoming month. This was not a request. Bloodshed was imminent and the Dhinnahs were seriously outnumbered. They had a fast family meeting and the small tax was paid right there and then. It was not the minor amount of money that was important. From this moment on the old loon was to some extent in charge, and the town had become at least loosely under our sway. The others paid up and in a sense they were paying for the thugs who were subjecting them to second-class status. The beauty of the thing: which worked out as I had hoped and planned, was that it was a bloodless coup. We might need every able bodied man in town to do God's work.

CHAPTER EIGHT

The Arablian Standoff

The Dhinnahs had paid and so had all the others but our rival cousins were furious. There was no problem the next month and I should have been on guard because they actually came to our saloon and paid in full a couple of days early. Arabia being Arabia the levels of treachery, double dealing, false promises, co-opting, conspiracies, shifting alliances and sudden murderous sneak attacks are always lurking around the oasis. The official story was that Fat Yusef had died of indigestion, but everybody knew he had been poisoned. A few days later, the second oldest brother was attacked by unknown assailants but only severely beaten. The third oldest brother Mustafa, known as Mustafa the Angry, emerged as the top Dhinnah and was quickly the undisputed leader of the clan. About ten days before the next constabulary tax was due the fourth oldest brother came back from the coast with an army of all Nubians from the lower Nile region. These thugs had reputations of being excellent with spears and knife fighting, but were generally not great camel riders.

The Dhinnahs made a demand that all the other families pay a defense tax to them.

This is where the standoff came in. The other families played both sides against the middle and refused to pay either us, or the Dhinnahs. If we attacked them they would run to the Dhinnahs and vice versa. The Dhinnah clan and we were approximately evenly matched and we just did not have the muscle to successfully go to war against them, or they against us for the same reason.

I had to change my tactics and try to obtain more money and also gain more people who believed that the old pervert was spouting the word of god. We also had to maintain our army because if we disbanded our group on Monday by Tuesday the Dhinnahs would be our lords and masters, and I would be on my back servicing about five camel jockeys an hour.

This is when I forged an alliance with the family of my old best customers the twins. Their family was mainly into the slave trade. It was generally easiest to obtain cheap slaves from the black areas across the Red Sea in Africa. Cheap slaves were always on demand because if they died from overwork, disease, or discipline it was no great loss. Stories abounded of families purchasing expensive specialized slaves who for one reason or another died with the owners being stuck with the loss.

Also, in the big slave markets of Khartoum and further south on the island of Zanzibar a huge number of slaves were always coming in because the different African tribes were always raising cash by capturing and enslaving neighbors. Middlemen would fan out with caravans of slaves to the Red Sea coast for resale. For reasons of monopoly and price control there was an Arabian wide agreement that only Arabs could bring slaves into Arabia and sell slaves in Arabia.

There was a lot of money to be made in importing cheap African slaves into Arabia and I wanted a piece of it.

Now, with their father's blessing, the twins were entering the business. That family had been in slave trading for generations and understood how it worked, but they needed capital. I, ostensibly through Mohammad's rambling, set up a joint venture where we would supply the working capital and they would bring in slaves, generally about 100 at a time, and we would split the profits. The older brother, Osama would stay in Mecca and take care of the Arabian end of the business while the younger brother Obama would go across the Rea Sea and take care of the African end.

I sent a small contingent across the sea with Obama to both keep an eye on our investment and also to see if we could get some converts to believe in the new prophet Mohammad. I had high hopes, but I knew the future was filled with uncertainty.

CHAPTER NINE

The Original Pillars of Islam

The first original pillar of Islam was the camel. Without Old Mama's well-timed buck, unsettling Mohammad's cranium, the movement would never have gotten off the sand. It was the camel, with mounted soldiers astride, which swelled our ranks of converts and territory by racing into villages and caravans, bloody scimitars in hand, installing fear and panic upon the unconverted. It was the lightning rapid expansion of Islam, dependent on these smelly, stupid beasts, which brought in the converts, territory, and booty that quickly established the religion, enlarged at the point of a menacing sword.

The second original pillar was the reason why those illiterate and slow to comprehend young murderous thugs were aboard those fleet and frightening large animals. It could be said more accurately, but I had my personal pithy shorthanded version, which in essence covered it. The second original pillar of Islam was alcoholism.

The ostensible founder Mohammad went from adolescence to death in a constant state of deep intoxication. But it was not his alcoholism that made the second pillar of Islam after all he was but the moronic, flatulent, figurehead. He was just there to be used at the beginning. The reason was that alcoholism was used to dull the senses of the mostly young, killing machines we put atop those camels to spread the religion once things got moving. Imagine being in a village, or oasis, or a caravan when 100 drunked up, dull-witted young thugs came charging with flashing steel blades flying high upon their rapidly closing camels. It is either surrender or to die a near instant death. The wiser ones immediately surrendered as the less wise were killed. The captive men where shackled and the after battle party was started with 90% of the surviving soldiers allowed to pollute themselves to total intoxicating senselessness, steal whatever they could hold in one hand, when it was vigorously shaken, and sexually possess any virgin, woman, boy, camel, sheep, or any other thing that had an orifice. It was the after battle party that made them want to go, with ferocious hell-bent excitement, into battle.

It was not only the booze, but also the whole panoply of intoxicants. Alcohol was just the most prevalent. We got these expendables hooked on everything. We had the hemp plant weed, the intoxicating chat from a locally grown plant that was chewed, and the betel nut that was grown nearby and was very inexpensive. We had poppies and the addicting opium that was derived from them. I wanted these men, actually mostly just older adolescents, to be dependent on getting their highs, getting used to the thrill and heart-pumping action of battle, as well as bullying those who had not converted to Islam. I made sure that these dummies were fed the warrior myths of paradise if they died in battle and they generally threw caution to the winds when they attacked. An army of fanatics, not afraid of death, can easily overwhelm a larger force made up of intelligent and cautious troops.

With those youngsters who looked like they could become leaders, we set up special training to turn them into adolescent fanatics. There was a small spot in the hills near the Red Sea, not all that far from Mecca, that was fairly lush and pretty. With these special boys, I called them the fruit of Islam, I would have a small contingent of them quietly slipped some numbing intoxicants that would put them into deep sleep. They would be transported to the special little valley where they would awake. In that valley would be fruit, sweet meats, alcohol, drugs, and especially pretty girls who were trained in the arts of male fulfillment. There were young boys for those who would prefer boys as well as musicians and lovely treats and tents. After several hours, they would again be drugged and brought back, while asleep, to Mecca. After they awoke they would start telling the wondrous tales of where they had been. These manboys would then be told that, as they were sleeping and dreaming, they were sent to the heavenlike paradise where great warriors go after death. They were informed that they had been chosen by God to glimpse what was in store for them because they were the specially chosen leaders.

The average chosen leaders and future officers sought great military careers and if death came quickly in battle then so be it, they were paradise bound for eternity. Some of the very brightest could see through the subterfuge, but kept it to themselves: and hoped they would get a second glimpse. Some of the bright ones, who were not quite smart enough to keep their doubts to themselves, were accused of some made-up infractions of rules and executed. Their buddies were told that by disobeying, these poor fellows lost paradise and would eternally wander and weep continuously in the afterlife, because they had thrown away the greatest gift that Allah could give - paradise.

CHAPTER TEN

The Cave

The Arabian standoff with the Dhinnahs was getting everybody absolutely nowhere. Here we are trying to cash in on the new religion, trying to make some serious money with the businesses and all we are doing is walking our camels in a circle. More money was coming in, but with the constabulary and some charitable work we had to do, we just were not progressing.

I had to see that everybody was helped out who professed belief in the glory of the drunken moron. I think some of the poor, older and disabled people used us because we had to place a safety net under the believers. A few believers were actually waylaid and killed by the Dhinnahs who wanted to do anything they could to undermine the religion. We had to protect our people as best we could and care for them or else the entire jig would be up.

The main problem was the exalted leader and Prophet. I took to studying other religions to get some new ideas. In the Christian Koran, they call it the Bible, it says that no man is a prophet in his hometown; this was definitely the case here. Before we could escape this dirty hellhole for another place, we needed money and people and a big army. We needed to get a start but it just was not happening, mainly because of Mohammad. We had proselytizers in other towns telling people of his greatness and wisdom. But in Mecca everyone knew what a flea bitten, foolish, old alcoholic he was. His words might sound great, but when he is laying in the middle of main crossroads dead drunk, with flies buzzing over his befouled clothing, it is hard to get people to believe he is the savior of mankind. This man was always covered with shit, vomit, piss, camelshit, spilled liquor, in short anything that was disgusting and smelled bad was his constant companion. The average camel was cleaner: it was a running joke and argument whether Old Mama or her master smelled worse. You can easily see that it was hard to sell this product as the word of wisdom and god.

So I decided I had to clean up the man and his image. I could generally talk him into almost anything, so I persuaded him to take a pilgrimage to Mount Hera. They have a lot of spooky-looking caves there and the place was remote. It was the type of place, a believer would think, where any god would feel at home.

The plan was to announce that god wanted to summons his number one boy to a cave for special instructions. In the meantime, and this went way back to the beginning, we were telling the populace how god works in mysterious ways and that regular people were incapable of understanding the ways of Allah. So we packed him off with a small retinue, which included me, to Mount Hera in an effort to put out a good spin. We had excellent provisions, tents, booze, and young girls and boys for him to screw. As he aged he seemed to be favoring boys more than women or girls, or even camels. We tried to keep him as clean as possible and one time we actually took him up to one of the caves for a quick looksee.

By the time we headed back I had the story of the miraculous cave and Mohammad's long one-on-one with the Angel Gabriel, who was Allah's conduit. The story was that he could not reveal everything, but that it was wondrous. All this came through my interpretations of his imbecilic trance babble. We cleaned him up and got him to promise (again) that he would slow down with the old behaviors.

It worked so well that I decided to make it an annual event. Slowly, very slowly, we were building up more believers. I assigned a contingent of guards to be with him at all times. They were to bring him home through flattery, requests, stealth, or force whenever he began to get drunk and real stupid.

CHAPTER ELEVEN

The Third Pillar of Islam

Like any movement, the she-camel's milk needed to nurture and grow Islam, was money. Without money nothing can be accomplished. Early in the quest to make Mohammad the most revered world leader, we were always in desperate need of more shekels. We needed shekels for troops, the believers, the proselytizers, the overhead, Mohammad's booze, and everything else. The old saying was and is that it takes shekels to make shekels.

Although we had our hand in many pots, trying to gain a profit for the prophet, the main income, the family's long time business, the third pillar of Islam is prostitution.

Men ruled the world, and certainly Arabia, and the easiest way to get men to part with their gold was through easily obtainable sex. No hassles, no preliminaries, no difficult dealing with the so-called weaker sex, just hand over your shekels and you get what you wanted, needed, and craved.

The world's oldest profession has always been lucrative and probably always will be. Otherwise normal, sane, and possibly sober men of wisdom, wealth and position, will mortgage their property and souls if a cute chippy sashays herself his way. This was the family business and we had been profiting with it for generations.

We first expanded with another joint venture with the twins' family. Osama turned out to be a natural pimp. We set up two satellite brothels with their help, that we controlled but they managed. The first was an operation like ours but a bit smaller and the second we placed in the low rent district aimed at the low class trade. Top prices were one shekel with bargain rates of a half shekel being possible.

The second of Osama's operations was what we called the bargain brothel. It was exclusively staffed by young Nubian slaves girls and turnover of the customers was very high, in and out. Turnover of the slave girls was equally high. If they lasted a month we had our investment back, if they lasted a year we made a small fortune and with the few that actually lasted five years we promised freedom and a trip back to Africa, if they wanted it. We did not do this out of the goodness of our hearts. Very few would endure the long hours, the constant stream of men, and the harsh discipline. But if they had hope of an eventual release from their personal hell, they would last longer.

We did not allow them to convert officially to the religion because even a moron could figure out that converting would greatly improve their lot. They were there to produce money, and that is what they did. Many died early and there was an occasional suicide, but the supply caravans carrying new brothel fodder was a continuous stream. The prices were sand cheap but the volume was high and the bargain brothel made good money.

We also decided to start a boys brothel outside of town. Here we had white slave boys between eight and sixteen working for us. We did this venture entirely ourselves under the ostensible overall management of the old drunk. We placed it out of town at a spot where non-believers had worshipped for centuries and got a steady flow of traffic.

The boys were mainly buggered anally, but all services were possible. There were no one shekel deals here; this was the high end of whoredom. Dealing with boys, the control and discipline had to be tight. We did find out that we did do better having the young charges intoxicated and continuously high. On special days when a crowd of horny men was likely to appear, we had a ritual to excite the customers.

There was this black rock at the center of our brothel that was just the right size for our leader to place a naked boy and anally enter the child. Others imitated Mohammad and the rock became a regular place to position the boys for sex.

On those specials days when the ritual was held, we dressed the boys up in loincloths that completely exposed their rears. They were made to wear sandals with wedges at the bottom that both made the boys taller and also made their rear ends wiggle more when they walked with the high sandals. We called the new footwear the scandal sandals. It got to be a tradition of the boys parading around the rock in their seductive bottom exposing clothing and manner, seven times counter-clockwise before the customers could make their choices. If two or more customers wanted a particular boy, a bidding war would ensue with the high bidder winning first dibs.

The habits I saw at this brothel revolted me; drunken men, screaming boys, and physical punishments that were barbaric; it was far worse than dealing with the women brothels. We did, however, make a ton of shekels at this perverted whorehouse and it became Mohammad's favorite. Also, when the boys got old enough to graduate out of the brothel, most of them gladly became part of our little army and they were fanatical soldiers looking to kill, destroy and humiliate the enemy. All by themselves they instilled fear into the infidels who had yet to embrace the Prophet. It was marvelous in how we profited from these boys in a way that allowed us to harvest and control their rage, as they became sociopathic, killing maniacs, spreading the joyous faith of Islam. It was really a wonderful thing we were doing, taking the enraged actions of homicidal stone-killing psychotics and turning it into useful, societally acceptable behavior.

Mohammad called his special rock the place of the golden anuses, because it was the anuses that brought in all the gold. In one of his trances at the boys brothel which was observed by several people, he kept on babbling the same nonsense collection of syllables. I used this word as Mohammad's name for his special Rock of the Golden Anuses, and this word has come down through the ages to modern times through my interpretation of his gibberish; the rock became know for all time as the Kaaba.

CHAPTER TWELVE

The Family Expands

With all my other troubles trying to coordinate the many aspects of starting a successful religion, the alleged Prophet complicated the situation by falling in love. This would not normally be a problem, he had certainly, at various times, gotten sweet on particular women, boys, camels and Allah knows what else. In his heyday before age and intoxicants got to him, he had quite a reputation as a man who was extremely virile. It was normally easiest to just indulge his fancy and fantasy, obtain his desire, and let nature take its course.

This time it was more complicated because his heart fell upon not a slave or whore, but a young nine-year-old girl from a good family who were honored as one of the first families to voluntarily embrace the faith. We needed this family, and families like them, and could not afford to offend the elders in any way. Telling Mohammad to lay off was totally useless, you could just as well talk to a large pile of camelshit for all the good it would do you. He was obvious and loud in his desire to sexually possess this child.

My head spun over the unbelievable gullibility of the girl's family when I found out that they actually felt honored that the Prophet had chosen their beloved little child for affection. I just could not believe it. Did their faith in Allah make them blind, that this lecherous, child-molesting, drunken, imbecilic pimp, full of filth, crud and evil smells, wanted to drool and fart over this innocent near baby. They wanted this decrepit grandfather, whom two thirds of the town only refrained from killing because our army of thugs kept the citizenry at bay, eyeing their little girl. This and other actions of the faithful were making it obvious to me that we were selling a very powerful product.

This did not mean, however, that he could just abduct her into the desert and attempt to rape her; he would have to marry her. You could not marry boys or camels, but in Arabia marrying a nine-year-old child was certainly no problem. The fact that my mother was still around, although she was beginning to look like she was 90 years old, was also of little consequence.

I hardly knew this girl, who was named Aisha. It was only after she became my stepmother that I realized what a moody, egotistical little bitch she was. Most children are sweet, but not this one. It did appear that she would evolve into a beautiful woman eventually, but she thought she was the jackal's pajamas at the age of nine. We took a mutual instant dislike to each other after she realized that I saw through all of her little games. She was an accomplished actress at a remarkably young age and was full of ambition and herself.

The only things beside herself that she loved were her mangy, old she-cat and her precious necklace that she had extorted as a wedding present. I was trying to hold the line on expenditures and she was the queen of need. She never wanted anything, but boy did she need things. Bringing her into the household was a real plus. The needy little she-devil actually did get the old fool to bathe a few times and wear unsoiled clothing on occasion, but you could see from her expressions what she thought of the ancient drunk. She would, at times, hold her nose and sit on his lap and make eyes at the old man, but if he seemed to be getting overly amorous she would always order more booze for him and get him into his normal catatonic state. She wanted old Mohammad on top of her about as much as I wanted a horny three-quarter ton camel on top of me.

I was able to use her to keep my dear old dad occupied and out of the public's eye to some extent, and also to clean him up a little, but it was very difficult having to deal with little miss precious.

He treated her more like a special granddaughter than a theoretical wife. I mean he screwed all his daughters so why not a granddaughter? This was the way the saloon & brothel worked with normal behavior but a distant memory and aberrant ways the norm. There was almost nothing that would have surprised or shocked me. All sorts of weirdos seemed to be attracted to us and Mohammed welcomed in every one who managed to cross our threshold. The hangers-on were not just weird but some were dangerously criminally insane. We had to kill a few who were too sick for even duty in our army of thuggish killers; that in itself tells you how far gone some of these men were. A few of the working girls had been horribly slashed or strangled, and some others were seriously beaten up. But the next day, if another cutthroat blew in fleeing from Allah knows where, because he was on the run from Allah know what, he would be welcomed in with open arms as one of the new boys. I always kept a dagger secreted in my sash and I would have used one in the blink of a lynx's eye.

I had to keep a rough tab on all these recruits. I made a game of it and tried to record a weekly list. Having a large number of these men around did instill a sober caution with our growing list of enemies, but at a great price. It seemed that word had spread that Mecca contained a place where anybody fleeing or seeking adventure could find a haven. Some more or less normal guys showed up, but they were the minority. I mentally separated the riffraff into five categories and this was important. I put the abnormal ones down as either: morons, drunks, sociopaths, fanatics, or thugs. It was hard to categorize some of them because there would be a guy who was a moronic, drunken thug, but I would choose a single label. We even had a few that could have arguably been in all five categories.

During a battle you would want the fanatics and socio-paths separated because they would attack each other instead of waiting for the enemy. An average weekly list would generally look like this: 22 morons, 71 drunks, 15 sociopaths, 22 fanatics, and 47 thugs. Additions for the week: 2 drunks, 1 sociopath, 1 fanatic, and 0 thugs with 1 less moron. The reason for the last entry was that the lead moron accidentally fell head first into the large well, the drunks tried to rescue him, but the sociopaths prevented the drunks from the rescue until after the moron was dead. This was a terribly disturbing setting that I had to deal with, I mean, no three ring freak show in history could rival this truly weird menagerie.

I cannot tell you how much I wanted to get things going in the right direction, rise above this perverted circus, and remove the seriously ill and dangerous from our immediate proximity. On more than a few occasions some drunk, generally harmless, but who knows, would wonder into my sleeping quarters looking for some action. You always had to keep your wits about you in this type of situation, and use your intelligence to romance them out. Thank Allah the whores were always available because these guys did not care too much who they tried to screw as long as something was handy with easy access. But who wants to be woken up by one of these burping assholes, often with their robes already unfastened. Believe me it was not a happy experience or pleasant sight. It took all my determination and resolve to remain sane within this loony bin of Allah.

CHAPTER THIRTEEN

The Gathering Storms

Life in Mecca was becoming intolerable. Basically the town was building up into two armed camps; the Mohammad lovers and the Mohammad haters. There were more haters than lovers but we did have a couple of advantages. The biggest advantage was that we were united. There was but one group of lovers, but the haters were divided into factions. The lead scoffers of Mohammad were still the Dhinnah family. Fortunately the slimy Mustafa the Angry, the head of the Dhinnah clan, was disliked almost as much as Mohammad. The fact that we were close cousins with the Dhinnahs also helped because it led some of the other families to question whether there was a ploy involved here, with our kinsmen the Dhinnahs being secretly allied with us. This was ridiculous on its face, but within the shifting Byzantine alliances and double-dealing of Arabia, it was at least plausible.

Another advantage we had was that many of our followers looked upon our figurehead leader as a Messianic divine conduit who was god's chief guy on earth. You could see it in their eyes when he would stumble past them. He was their conductor to eternal bliss. I did everything I possibly could do, to keep him under wraps, but I could not jail him or put him under any restraints, he was the Messenger.

As a tactic, when we were pretty sure that one of the faithful was truly and sincerely devoted, and also not a great warrior, who was needed for the muscle end of the movement, I would assign the devout follower to a different city or town to proselytize the unconverted. This was dangerous work and we lost a percentage to murder, but many were successful and converted infidels. The average convert was likely to become a believer when they were in a difficult personal crisis. The bigger the problems of the potential convert, the more chance of success. We would convert anybody: women, slaves, elderly peasants or if possible, we would get the plum converts- the leading citizens. Anyone could become in some way useful, but the rich and powerful were more useful. Faith in the prophet worked its magic in unusual ways.

There was a problem with some of the proselytizers. They were generally somewhat unstable when they found peace in Islam. Islam means submission in the sense that the devotee submits to Allah through the teachings of the Prophet. The idea is to get the person to accept as fact that he or she knows nothing and will submit to take orders from us. It helped that we were in the brothel business for years and years, because we used the same strategy with the problem whores and turnouts. You have to get them to accept their lot and to follow orders without question or thought. But the difficulty working with some of the ones who buy on hook, line, and sinker is that we were dealing with troubled, borderline personalities who were searching for an answer to their own and the world's problems. We do provide the answers. We provide the answers in the form of a drunken piss-laden old fool and some of them buy it, and through Mohammad find their own personal peace.

However, being unstable to begin with, these people were capable of changing their minds on a minute's notice for any reason. I could tell of several cases where blindly faithful good people, who had gladly and fervently devoted years of great service spreading the joyous news, viciously turned on us, violently biting the hand that had been nurturing them. These people had inside information on how we operated and could truthfully paint an accurate picture of the shortcomings of the man Allah picked as his Prophet.

We had a head person in every region that we sent devotees to spread Allah's word. We called these people our 'caravan leaders'. We made sure that the caravan leaders knew that if any of the proselytizers looked like or, in fact, did turn against us, they had to be immediately neutralized. Nothing, is worse than your former guy telling the same potential converts that it is all a pack of lies and distortions. We moved the caravan leaders every so often so they would not get too comfortable in their new territory and we had a secret number two caravan leader, known only to the leadership in Mecca, whose only job was to watch the number one caravan leader.

Because of our knowledge gained by running brothels, we were generally able to keep one step ahead of our own people. Things follow patterns when you deal with psychologically unstable personalities, and if you do not plan and follow up with actions, the movement will suffer. We had enough problems trying to keep everything together, without worrying about a whole bunch of loud turncoats exposing us to ridicule and reversing the hard fought fieldwork.

Sending missionaries out to the hinterland was an essential element. It was in a sense hit or miss, but in the larger long viewed way of looking at things, it was very successful. We would even gain entire families or towns if we could get the local chief to see the light. The biggest problem was that after conversion many of the important people, who had the means to travel, wanted to meet Allah's Messenger.

CHAPTER FOURTEEN

The Jew of Mecca

There was a certain Jew of Mecca, named Aaron the Wise, who had a much larger role in the founding of Islam than almost anybody realized. He was some years older than my father Mohammad, but because Aaron lived a much more sober and healthy life, Aaron looked younger and more virile. I had known Aaron from infancy and he took a slight interest in me, when I showed my juvenile promise, and asked if I could speak Hebrew with him. At the time, my Hebrew was very limited, but he was amazed and helped me learn the language and how it was written. He had business dealings with my father and I saw him about once a week. He always showed great respect and kindness toward my mother.

From an early age, Aaron was the leader of the small Jewish community of Mecca until his death many years later. His main business was money lending, but he had other interests as well. The Jews were tolerated in Mecca, but they were generally disliked and not trusted by most of the families. They mainly kept to themselves and never intermarried, but some of the men did have non-Jewish mistresses, from time to time, who were generally servant girls or slaves. Often, if a child was born out of one of these affairs, the child would be adopted into the tribe and treated as a full free Jew from that moment onward.

My father and Aaron had dealings as Aaron did with other leading clansmen of the various Meccan families. When a person wanted to borrow money, the rate was generally two and one-half percent a month or 25% per year for interest. Aaron would have the money to lend, but being an outsider, if Aaron just lent the money, the borrower would never pay it back. How the business worked was that technically Mohammad would lend the money to one of Mohammad's retainers and Aaron would just service the debt as Mohammad's agent. This was a fiction that everyone understood, but the borrower had to repay the loan or be in Mohammad's debt. This would have meant that the debtor's property would be seized and family sold into slavery if the debt was not repaid. Mohammad would reap some of the profit from the loan just by being the figurehead. Mohammad seemed to be good at profiting in life by merely being a figurehead.

All the families made money in this way and we did receive several girls who entered our brothels as virgin turnouts when their profligate fathers got over their heads in debt. They sold their daughters to avoid bankruptcy and total ruin. The fathers always promised that they would redeem their daughters when the money problems were over, and made a big deal of negotiating a redemption price, but to my knowledge it never happened, not even once. After the religion started we had to sever the business relationship with Aaron because we could not enslave any of our own believers, or be too closely allied with the hated moneylenders, which would be bad for the god business.

On occasion Aaron would use the services of one of the brothel girls, but he would never chose me in that long year when I was a brothel inmate. He was the only male in Mecca who did not screw me out of respect, because we had a non-whore/trick relationship. He was called Aaron the Wise because he was learned and he especially understood numbers. He taught me some numbers and was pleased with my progress; he was much more proficient than my original teacher Ra'hel had been.

I also knew, in early childhood and beyond, his daughter Naomi. She was a few months older than I and she also had the reputation of being very beautiful. Naomi would never be allowed into our complex or any other, which held a saloon & brothel, but I saw her when I was allowed to visit Aaron's household. I played with Naomi and she was very much like me, except that she was Jewish and was expected to remain a virgin, a real full virgin, until she would marry a Jew. She prayed that her father would choose her distant cousin, Elijah, from Medina to be her bridegroom: she was forever telling me how handsome and smart he was.

Aaron gave me a numbers problem that he said he would

ask me about after one week's study. He asked me: if a money lender had no expenses, and lent out 1000 shekels for 20 years at either 2% a month or 25% a year and could lend out the money that came in as interest at the same rate (he called this compounding), approximately how many shekels would the money lender have at the end of the 20 year period? I eagerly studied the problem and had the answer in two days. When I saw him a week later he wanted to know my answer. I proudly told him that I had studied the problem and figured it out in different ways and that the answer always came out to be about 100,000 shekels or 100 shekels for each original one. He was very pleased with me.

He gave me some books in Hebrew on numbers and I studied them, they helped me grasp the magic of numbers. It also helped me understand the power of money; I just needed to obtain more so the movement could flourish before the many problems of Mecca would destroy it.

CHAPTER FIFTEEN

The Fourth Pillar of Islam

The four pillars of Islam, the founding supports that were needed in order that the religion could flourish, grow, and conquer, were the essentials. The first three were the camel, alcoholism, and prostitution. The fourth and last pillar, the final original building block needed to complete the quartet that enshrined Islam, was the pillar of mental illness.

I could have called the final pillar aberrant mental functioning, or delusions, or several other terms, but in my short hand way of describing the needed elements, to insure that Islam became what is has become, I simply called the last pillar, mental illness.

There were and are various elements or levels of the mental illness which nursed Islam from its infancy to this modern era. In a sense, the second pillar of alcoholism, within its sphere of all the intoxicants and hallucinogens, is a form of mental illness in that the unaffected, sober, clear thinking mind is brought to a state of confusion and illogic. Decisions made while drunk or in a narcotic haze generally are not wise. Similarly, recruiting an army of warriors from those who were severally twisted in childhood and adolescence by constant psychotic and delusional episodes allowed our army to fight with a fanaticism and cruelty that so cowered our conquests that we were able to achieve outstanding victories with lightning speed. No sane person wants to confront homicidal, blood thirsty warriors, scimitars in hand, who easily would welcome death, and its guarantee of paradise, our savage and savaged warriors were worth their weight in gold. The early pitched battles of Badr and Yarmouk were won by the beatings, cruelty and rapes at the Kaaba.

But the greatest power of the pillar of mental illness, the essential ingredient necessary to nurture Islam, was a more general and all-powerful element of this malady. To put it another way, we were able to accomplish something that is difficult to truly comprehend. We used fear, torture, love, kindness, magic, mystery and wonderment along with gullibility, yearning and faith. We were able to tap into man's innate need for deathlessness. We bridged the gap into the human mind and connected with the primordial, psychological imperative of the number one fear of humankind. This mass delusion, set up within the confines of the law and harsh punishment, was able to blind rational people to believe the irrational. Eventually, we were able to have sane human beings believe that a man they knew as a drunken, lecherous old fool, full of cam-elshit and fleas, was the Prophet of Allah. This man, one of the least among them, was the conduit to the all power-ful, all knowing, all everything of Allah. Allah who was the entity responsible for miracles, knowledge, love, hate, war, life, death, and salvation.

We convinced them to believe that the superintendent of the universe chose Mohammad as His agent. This grand delusion, that everything was solvable; all problems, real, imagined, futuristic or impossible, and solvable by faith in this urine-soaked, camel-breathed lunatic. All of this because of man's deep seated, instinctive fear of death. We were able to get huge numbers of otherwise normal people, to believe the unbelievable by promising the one thing mankind desires most, desires to the point of life-long obsession, the need and hope of everlasting life. By hawking this product, we were able to get people to sac-rifice their earthly lives, their property, and their families. And what did they get in return, they got Allah, Allah, who was hard to understand, but who would shepherd them to heaven so they could live forever, after they expired from this world.

With relish, I turned normal people into semi-fanat-ics. I marveled at my own powers of manipulation. Allah, Allah, everything was Allah, and his number one boy, the exulted Mohammad. As the movement grew using our four building blocks, the legends and myths soared into fantasy. If anyone disagreed, then it would be an early and cruel death to the counter-revolutionary, the blasphemous scoffer, the anti-Allah.

We had the word of Allah. This was unchallengeable. We could kill for Allah, torture for Allah, and enslave for Allah. A man could dislike his neighbor, speak ill of his neighbor, or act against his neighbor; but you could never dislike, speak or act against Allah. By definition it was impossible, unless you were the worst of the worst, someone who demanded a swift ignominious death. From infancy to dotage, every authority figure, institution, and holy man preached the same sermon and sang the same mantra. Submit to Allah. If Allah did something that seemed cruel or wrong, it was just that you were too ignorant to understand. Only Allah understands, and he moves in mysterious ways that ordinary people could never comprehend. You must submit. The greatest product ever sold: the illusion from nothingness, the illusion of Allah.

CHAPTER SIXTEEN

My Cousin Ali

There was a certain individual whose life and mine were always intertwined. My cousin Ali and I were brought up in the same crazy household, only he took to it like a thirsty camel to cool, clear oasis water. He was my father's favorite, and young Ali idealized the old fool. Imitation is the sincerest form of flattery, and Ali always wanted to be the younger clone of Mohammad. They were far from identical, but Ali certainly and sincerely worshipped his elder kinsman. More than any other human being, Ali was devoted and totally loyal to our drunken Messenger. It was a town-wide joke that there was no cliff high enough in the world that Ali would not gladly follow Mohammad over. Needless to say, Mohammad loved his little lap puppy; who could so easily see the Prophet's greatness.

Ali showed some strange dualisms and paradoxes. Ali was a cherubically good looking youngster who away from his mentor would enjoy cleanliness, good grooming, and even perfume, but at Mohammad's lead he would gladly roll head first into camelshit and puke. He distanced himself from all other evil smelling camelmen, but his nose knew no problems when his old cousin was around. It was a very odd thing, as if two people inhabited the same body, the clean and the disgustingly filthy. Ali was not only the most loyal adherent to our leader, but also the first of the true believers in Mohammad's sanctity.

Ali was special to the sonless Mohammad in many ways. When the drunken, exalted leader would feel the urge, he would, no matter where, or in front of whom, strip Ali and anally enter the boy. As Ali grew older and the drunken lifestyle of Mohammad took its toll, Ali would harden the old master first so he could be buggered. But no one else, no matter how rich or powerful, could enjoy Ali's ass. This is what both Mohammad and Ali wanted. Ali was the exclusive boy toy of his calabash Dad. From Ali's standpoint it was a marriage of purity, love and truth.

Needless to say, I could never stomach the little sicko wimp. It was the complication of one more weird, seriously delusional, and totally sick individual, with which I had to contend . Also, Ali did nothing to clean up His Filthiness or improve his cousin's reputation.

The two of them were a walking scandal, and more fodder for the scoffers and haters. I gave serious thought of having Ali meet with an unfortunate accident or illness, but it might have complicated things even more. If nothing else, Ali was predictable, constantly singing the praises of Islam, and how happy he was because of the understanding and presence that Mohammad brought. All in all, he might have been a small plus to the movement, the only real problem was that whenever he entered the room, I always felt an immediate overwhelming urge to vomit. The little cocksucker, and in Ali's case it was literal, just turned my stomach.

For many, many years I was astonished at the fact of my sanity within the hellish pandemonium of my family. I just could not understand why I was the only one in the family who was sane, sober, and smart; at times I feared retrogressing into the madhouse of Mohammad. It was a sobering thought that made me focus on the future.

CHAPTER SEVENTEEN

The Deteriorating Situation in Mecca

As time wore on the tension of the standoff took its toll. The Mohammad haters were foaming at the mouth, but our many loyal adherents and thugs kept them at bay. If absolutely nothing happened, nature would take its course, Allah would eventually call Mohammad home, and the movement might then possibly fizzle out to an inglorious death. We needed to reach a critical size before that event, in order that the religion would be strong enough to survive Mohammad.

Things were quickly coming to a boil in Mecca. With our expansion into liquor importation, our rival kinsmen, the Dhinnahs, had more or less decided to risk open armed conflict and kill the Messenger. It became apparent that we had to waste more assets constantly guarding our wandering drunk, because his premature death could really hurt us, perhaps to the point of total destruction. Both sides of the standoff, or actually the three factions: us, the

Dhinnahs, and the neutrals, who played both sides for their own advantage, all had spies. We had to execute several suspected spies, after we tortured them, to find out whom they worked for, and the names of their confederates.

We had the best intelligence, and it steered the course of history. Many people became spies for different reasons, such as greed, hatred of masters, thrill seekers, egomaniacs, and other various things. But the greatest reason was the belief that the spy was working for eternal salvation. When we converted people who were privy to inside information in other families, they became our secret members. This saved them from lash-happy masters, who definitely would disapprove, but more importantly it gave us ears within the inner sanctums of our enemies. A person did not have to be important to learn things, a cook or water boy could hear many things. We even used counter-measures when we discovered or suspected that we had a spy in our midst. We would feed that person misinformation: such as a neutral family was secretly siding with us, or that a powerful tribe outside of Mecca was in negotiations to convert.

All of a sudden, our intelligence network was awash with disturbing news. These incoming packets of information, from so many different sources, and from such a wide area, almost had to be true. It was the absolutely worst possible news. Our enemies had decided to assassinate me.

Mohammad still went into his authoritarian trances, although a little less often, but he was usually, but not always, removed from the general vicinity of casual observers and listeners. A few times, some people put out trial balloons that they were beginning to be able to understand his wild ranting. This was more nonsense than the wild rambling utterances themselves, the would-be interpreters were either delusional or fraudulent. It did not matter much whether it was fraud or fancy. I let them know, quickly and firmly; that I was told by Allah through his mouthpiece the drunken fool, I would be the only one to ever have the gift. And we all know how Allah does not like to be contradicted by mere mortals, the key word being mortals, if you get my meaning.

Now our enemies wanted me very quickly dispatched to paradise. No one could ever figure out that I was the puppet master pulling the strings of Islam. I was fully revirginated by this point, but my enemies still looked upon me as a pretty, but insignificant young girl; capable of nothing meaningful. Most of the town fathers had even humped me in my old two and three shekel days, and that made me, in their eyes, an even more insignificant little chippy. But they knew that if I were dead then there would be no more wise sayings and a gigantic blow would be dealt to the movement.

Mohammad was still saying very wise things and we were obviously getting loyal and devoted converts, a fact our enemies found very dangerous. Even some of the, generally younger, members of the leading families became enamored with Islam. The opposition found this fact horribly disturbing, it was almost as if we had killed these children of theirs. In a sense the upcoming clouds of war foreshadowed a civil war, a conflict that could be fought brother versus brother.

Without question I had to take immediate action before my assassination. Medina was a city that had a lot of our followers. Some of our best proselytizers had been assigned there, and they had established a fifth column of adherents in the city. Medina had a large Jewish contingent, was used to multi-factions, enjoyed a long-standing general truce between all parties, and they now existed happily in a live and let live community. I decided it was time to blow Mecca off and head to the greener oasis of Medina.

But you must emanate strength before a move like this can be made. If you show weakness or fear, you will be cut down faster than a very lame old camel. I put out the spin that Medina was inviting Mohammad and all his followers to their city. We allegedly were to enter as honored guest, with Mohammad being figuratively given the key to the city. These were desperate times for the movement. Allah, speaking through the Prophet, let all his disciples know these facts. Our actions did freeze our enemies, who just wished we left to go anywhere else in the world, and hopefully in a hurry. Mohammad arranged through me, the sale of all our businesses and real estate. They were at almost fire sale prices, but we were able to liquefy them for some gold. We had some of our secret converts stay stealthily behind as we made our preparations for the escape to Medina

As I planned the move, I knew we wished to avoid any armed conflict. We needed every hand because if we came to Medina in strength, we had a much better chance of being allowed to stay there in peace. I did not want to be like the ancient Israelites wandering in this damn desert for the next forty years.

CHAPTER EIGHTEEN

Preparations

Logistically I knew that it was going to be a mess; I could handle a mess, what I could not handle was a debacle. I decided to consult with Aaron the Wise, probably the smartest man in Mecca. He certainly was conversant with everything that was happening, as well as having contacts, through his money lending business, with every leading family in town. Thankfully, I had a great relationship with him and a mutually respectful friendship. Also, he was familiar with Medina and in close contact with the powerful Jewish leadership there.

He told me that he had expected my visit and would gladly help me. I had sent a servant over in the morning to ask permission to make a noontime call, which was automatically welcomed. But Aaron asked if he could be excused for about one hour because of a previous business commitment, and if I could visit with his daughter Naomi until then. I was glad to see Naomi, and she was wildly happy. Her cousin the handsome man of her dreams, Elijah, from Medina, was in town. She confided in me that being 22 years old, she was ready for marriage and felt the desire to lose her virginal status. I was but some months younger than she was, and I told her that men could be interesting, but that they were generally no big deal. I personally had received a few men here and there in the last few years, when I felt the desire, but I had gone as long as a year at a time without them. I liked the fact that I was now revirginated, and it was so much better than those long ago days of servicing anybody and everybody for short money.

Now Naomi, a lovely girl in every way, was a little on the sheltered and naïve side. What could you expect from a wealthy, pretty, Jewish girl, whose powerful father treated her as a queen, and who at 22 was still a true virgin, who had never ever once slept with a man. I really liked her, but she could rattle on, and especially on her favorite subject, the handsome, good looking, great looking, charming, etc. Elijah. I thought that if she ever actually got alone with Elijah, her elegant silken wraparounds would hit the floor faster than the hooves of a racing camel. Naomi, was not only ready for Elijah, she was in heat.

Now I had never met this Elijah, but I expected some intellectual, wimpish creature worried about this, that, and everything else. Several of the younger Jewish men I had met, including Naomi's two brothers, were on the namby-pamby side fretting about the weather, fleas, their skin and having a whole host of minor problems. Then Elijah showed up and all I could say was "Wow!" What emerged as he strolled in was a finely chiseled, rakish, strong, confident dreamboat who glided through the air with a smile and a twinkle that just exuded sex appeal. Suddenly, Naomi did not seem like quite such a twit. This guy was hotter than the Arabian Desert sands at high noon during the solstice. I had not been taken aback, like this, in years. In the old days I would have gladly lent him three shekels, and have given him the ride of his life. When Elijah presented himself Naomi seemed to enter a Mohammad-like trance, only she appeared to be mute. Her eyes just gazed with her smile ear to ear. Elijah came in very shortly before Aaron, so I had to leave the chaperoned young couple, but I had certainly changed my tune over this young Nimrod.

I had to mention to Aaron how Naomi was certainly impressed by Elijah's charms. "Don't tell me, I hear it 50 times a day" was his answer. Old Aaron said that with luck a wedding announcement may be coming soon, but there were still some points that had not quite been negotiated yet.

We then discussed the important business. He definitely gave me some ideas that I put into practice. I wanted to flee Mecca as fast as a camel could trot, because nothing good was going to happen while we were still stuck in that hellhole. We had to be cautious, but we also had to scramble. Time was of the essence and it was the moment to make history. In a sense, the flight from Mecca to Medina was a make or break moment for Islam. No man is a Prophet in his own city, but now we were exiting the old and running to a new place, which might help us accomplish everything we desired. We were heading to a city in which he might truly be adored as a Prophet, a place where he was mostly known by the praises sung by our people. In short, it was my hope that Islam could now truly begin and flourish. I knew that from this point on, it was imperative to keep Mohammad's drunken, boorish behavior hidden from the many peering eyes of Medina.

CHAPTER NINETEEN

The Flight to Medina

I sent an advance party to Medina to smooth the way for the large contingent that was coming. Fortunately, Aaron the Wise was going to Medina on business with his prospective son-in-law, Elijah, and he promised to let the Jewish leadership know that we were coming and that we would come in peace and not looking to upset any fig stands. I promised him that we had no problems with the Jews; we just wanted to be allowed to live in peace, away from the turmoil and hassles of Mecca. It was true that we had gotten a few, not many but a few, Jewish converts, but we were not targeting Jews for conversion. At that nascent point of Islam, all people were welcome: rich and slave, old and young, smart and dumb, we were as welcoming to converts as my old brothel was to a weary and horny caravan.

I split our organized thugs into two contingents. One was at the lead of our group, and the other lagged behind at the rear. Periodically the front end would stop to let the rear catch up. We never wanted our split constabulary to be too far apart. I had also sent provisioning teams to designated oases, to have the needed material there when the people's army arrived. The long march was difficult and time consuming, and it was especially difficult on the old. We had to bury the fallen in the sand; there was no other way. My largest fear, of an attack never materialized. We only lost people because of the inhospitable desert, as we crossed the vast wasteland of death, heat, and despair of my homeland. The trip is only about 200 miles, but it was slow trudging in difficult terrain. We generally were on the move twice daily, in the hours before and after dawn, and also in the hours around dusk. It was too painfully hot around midday, and the people and animals needed the cool rest time during the night. On the whole, we did remarkably well considering the obstacles that we faced. Arabia can kill and our people, when we did finally finish, loudly thanked Allah and his Prophet.

The first major test, the first giant hurdle was passed. As we like to say on the peninsula, we were out of the desert, which was true, literarily and figuratively. As a movement, we were entering the second phase, hopefully the first stable and possibly expansionist stage. We had been terribly vulnerable in Mecca, and subject to massacre during the escape, but we made it with as little wear and tear as possible. I would have thanked Allah myself, if she could have possibly existed.

The main necessary step here was to keep the old drunk as hidden as practicable. He was too well known to have him killed and a sane and sober replacement put in his place. We were stuck with him, and in a sense needed him to be around longer, so his body of wisdom could grow to a respectful length. I put in many of my few spare hours into authoring his sayings and his wisdom. The one thing we did not need, and what would destroy us, was his normal habits becoming widely known. You could clean him up, but like a child, ten minutes later he would manage to befoul his pants, vomit, and be scrambling in the dirt chasing a nine year old slave boy. It looked foolish, and was too amusing, when single digit aged slave boys would twist, turn and struggle in an effort to free themselves from his sexual advances. This was the guy I had to raise to be the most respected man in Arabia; he did not make it easy.

Choosing him, as spiritual leader was not a mistake, it just seemed that way. It was, in fact, the only way. I needed an important local man that I could easily manipulate, and one too intoxicated and stupid to figure out that he was but a marionette on a string. He was the only choice I had and the circumstances were almost providential. Early on, things fell into place as if guided by the cosmos. I saw my opportunities and I seized them.

The problem was that I needed a drunken moron, and then I had to deal with, manage and guide a drunken moron. It was not easy taking this pig of a man and making him out to be a prince. Thank Allah for the gullibility of man and especially for the gullibility of the Arabian man. Without these easily fooled, camel loving dullards, the religion would not have survived the first sand storm, and I knew that there were many more sand storms on the way.

CHAPTER TWENTY

Settling Down

We got settled and opened up some brothels aimed at different slices of the sex trade. Obama sent over a large contingent of African chippies for our cut-rate operation, and we opened up a couple of higher-class joints, and two boys brothels. I decided to expand the boy trade because they not only made good money, but we needed those wonderful warriors who graduated when the youths outgrew their cuteness. I would bring boys to Mohammad rather than letting Mohammad always go to the boys. The last place I wanted the Prophet to be constantly was at the boys brothels, making a total asshole of himself. That was what the boys were for, not him. I decided to put Ali nominally in charge of the smaller one, which was the physically farthest away from me. I mean he was there everyday anyway, so I was able to legitimize it, and with his sadistic tendencies he would help the future fruit of Islam emerge from the degradation of pain, humiliation and sadism, to the joys of being Allah's elite savage and crazed killing machines.

Just as a wise camel owner gets everything he can from

his beast: meat, milk, leather, soup bones, and transport, and sometimes even love; we get money and then useful deaths to our enemies from these boys. The major problem was that they generally, because of the nature of their sociopathic fanaticism, went too quickly to paradise, often within two years of enlistment. The few that survived to middle age made wonderful, fearful commanders. We tried to foster the idea that the longer you faithfully served Allah on earth the better paradise would be. It might be an obvious oxymoronic concept, ridiculous on its face, but to an illiterate, sociopathic, addicted manboy with a twisted psyche and tortured soul, it makes sense. Believe me I know.

We were at peace with our neighbors, making good money, sending our drummers out proselytizing; it was now time to start war on those infidels who had not yet had the wisdom to see the fulfilling peace of Islam. Islam means surrender, and we needed territory and people to bring in the capital to fuel our war machine. It was a business decision; you attacked a settlement, obtained converts, slaves, money, animals, etc. and if it only cost you a few soldiers, it was a profitable day. The young men who converted rather than die could then be conscripted into our army of thugs, and be in the attack of the next village, killing their cousins if necessary. When it worked, it worked well.

I just needed a little more time to build up our money, troops, and adherents, and then I could begin the major expansion. The beauty of our movement was that we were not just everyday conquerors; no, we were doing this for salvation, for Allah. Wherever we would go, our advance men would have already been there, spreading the good news about Allah and his revered Messenger, Mohammad. We had our own little fifth column in every hamlet, oasis, and even in almost every caravan. We told our people that if there was ever a problem and our soldiers were attacking, our followers were to place their hands over the tops of their heads with the fingers together and pointing upwards. Some non-converts would imitate this action when they saw that the killing fanatics would pass over these people without harming them. This was fine, these people were smart enough to see the big picture and immediately say they were converting. The goal was to get territory and adherents. The more people supporting you, and the fewer throwing stones, made these raids much easier and with fewer thug casualties.

That wonderful, relatively quiet, interlude between the hell of Mecca and the danger of the escape, contrasted with the upcoming wars, was that period of time that my inner soul so badly needed. I drank in the cold, sweet waters of calm peace and prosperity like a newborn cub camel taking his first draughts of warm mother's milk. The fairy boy Ali was mostly out of my hair and sight, dear old dad was drinking and screwing his fill mostly in privacy, and the shekels and converts were coming in. If it were not for the damn driving ambition I now understood I was cursed with, I could have taken an easier track of contented peace with a good man and start a normal family and live the good life. My existence was so full of problems and time constraints, that I needed a rest if I were to fulfill my destiny and birth Islam into this world. It was so tempting that I decided to compromise a little bit and do something for Fatima. The movement would be there; perhaps the idiots could keep it going for centuries. It was okay, I reckoned, to selfishly let myself enjoy a bite of the shish kabob. I was after all a mature, but chronologically young woman, I needed to be held, caressed, and loved. I needed to reconnect with my feminine side, how badly I needed to be told that I was beautiful.

CHAPTER TWENTY-ONE

The Man of My Dreams

As Aaron the Wise went back to his home city of Mecca, I restrained myself until he was atop his camel and the animal had taken three strides south. I had a great relationship with Aaron and I did not want to queer it in any way. Aaron had big news for his daughter Naomi, negotiations were concluded and the marriage contract signed, Elijah was to be her bridegroom at a grand wedding in Mecca in only six months. Finally an end to her hated extra virginity was in sight. Aaron was going home to let Naomi know that her prayers had been answered and his leaving was the answer to my secret desires.

Elijah was sizzling hot and I knew that we could both reach total personal satisfaction in steamy, intertwined, mutual rapture. I had to see if this polished stud would live up to his billing. I had to really keep it cool, but I did notice that he certainly, like most men, gave me more than the once over. I had to use every scintilla of discipline to keep my outward desires in check, but I am sure I succeeded. It had been about a decade since I was a baby whore screwing every Tamir, Dharr, and Habib who wandered in from the desert with two or three shekels. I was officially fully revirginated, but I still understood men; nothing, and I mean nothing, will wise a girl up to the vanities, inner fears, and needs of men than screwing twenty different guys a shift for money. If that does not school a girl on how to get what she wants from a man, then she is hopeless. What I wanted was to see if this dreamy Adonis would give me the warmth, desire, caresses, sympathy and love that I craved. I needed the physical, but I hungered for the emotional connection that only a man can impart to a woman. I had horribly lost my physical maidenhead a decade ago right before my twelfth birthday; I was now happily ready to lose my emotional virginity.

Like everybody else within this sand blown peninsula, Elijah knew that every female in Mohammad's household had been a whore. This would probably make it easier to physically couple, but harder to reach the mutual respect and equality I wanted, so that we could, perhaps on a long term basis, reach a true loving blissful togetherness. Marriage would not be impossible, but very difficult and the wife always had to convert to the husband's god. Since I absolutely could not do that and still stay in the new religion, it was impossible unless he converted to Islam first. There were so many practical problems that it was totally unlikely that we could ever get legally married.

I was putting the camel before the caravan here, but even if he turned out to be the absolute perfect guy for me, it would have to be a rear of the tent relationship.

I invited him over to discuss some minor business as soon as Aaron was heading south, and had a long talk with him. If I threw myself at him I would lose all his respect. He was a Jew, but a man is a man whatever faith he professes.

I congratulated him on his approaching nuptials and his entrance into the prominent family of Aaron. After a while, I let him know that even with my unusual position as interpreter of the Prophet's wisdom; and being an unmarried technical virgin, that I believed in gender equality and was against the many Arabian rules that subjugated women to their fathers and then their husbands. He smiled and readily agreed. It was obvious that he would like to get into my wraparounds. I put up the obligatory resistance until I finally let him ravish me. Everything that I hoped and dreamed about emerged as he skillfully rode me to rapture. Wow, I felt that I had moved to a new, higher physical level than I had never before reached, while forging a deep spiritual bond of oneness. It was so nice to have a clean, good smelling, handsome man, one I really liked, inside me. What a change from my former existence. Now I certainly knew that men could change their attitude ten seconds after ejaculation. But my sweet, lovely, honey of a dreamboat guy, elongated my joy with sensitive, amorous talk and physical togetherness after the blissful climax. Boy, did I like this guy. Naomi, lucky for her, would never know the rough unpleasant side of coupling. She would only have sex with this wonderman, I could explain a lot to her, but she would be so much better off just sleeping with this kind, sensitive hunk, a man's man, who deeply understood how to treat a woman.

With each bated breath, as I lay softly next to Elijah in post coital coziness, I tingled, as I quietly felt so alive. Gone was the time when I hated sex, the endless continuous chore of one fool after another pawing, probing, and manhandling my juvenile body. I vowed that the inter-family pimping would end with me, and that my children would be raised like Naomi's, not being forced to degrade and humiliate themselves as playthings for the lust of smelly morons. How I hated the old horrible fool who had fathered me and then cruelly pimped me out. The images of my evil father faded quickly from my mind as I again thought of the wonderful Elijah, my beautiful prince who would protect me from evil.

I prayed that this encounter would be the beginning of a new reinvented Fatima, the engorged satisfied young woman, the happy girl finally loving life.

CHAPTER TWENTY-TWO

Peaceful Interlude

My life took on its first sustained pleasurable period. Elijah seemed to be as wildly happy with me as I was with him. We got together for business every day as I had hired him as the movement's liaison to the Jewish community. A deal was made with the elders of the Jewish tribe that we would not proselytize to any Jews. If a Jew decided on his own to convert, we would not take him or her unless the elders got a chance to counsel the prospect and try to dissuade him. Only after a reasonable period in which the person would loudly and continuously insist that they wanted to leave Judaism would we take the person in. We agreed to have no secret Jewish converts. This limited our inroads to get Jewish converts, but strengthened our position with the powerful Jewish forces. Elijah always insisted, when asked, that he was born Jewish and would die Jewish, that he just had a job with the movement to make sure that no misunderstandings developed.

We talked a lot about everything, and he was like his kinsman and future father-in-law Aaron, a very wise man. I promised him that Islam would work with the Jews and that both groups would get stronger if they remained in mutual harmony. About this time, as always, Mohammad was adding to the wisdom of what became the Koran. I had set it up so that many contradictory things would be in there, as all the holy books I was familiar with were written. Now, more things were put in about getting along with your neighbors, and Islam's special relationship with the people of the book. I had set it up that both the old and new testament of the Bible were revered as ancient written wisdom, which Mohammad built upon as Allah's number one Prophet. The contradictory sayings would allow me, or any future leader grounds to do what we wanted by selectively quoting whatever passage favored our position.

Elijah was going to be bringing his bride Naomi back to Medina after the wedding. I could stand him being away for the wedding and honeymoon, but we both wanted to be able to continue the wonderful thing we had together. I could share him; I just could not give Naomi an exclusive.

Even with all the money and converts coming in, the blissful interlude was doomed, because the wars would have to start. However, I delayed things somewhat because I had never been so happy. Elijah and I had to be discreet, but this was not that difficult. Mohammad was slowing down a little bit more, which certainly made my life a lot easier. As long as boys and booze, with a little food, were brought his way, he was satisfied in his fool's paradise. I began to set up a plan for our expansion.

The first thing I hoped to do was to divide Medina into two adjoining and allied parts. We would control our half and everyone in it, and our allies the Jews would have their half. Actually the Jews would have more like a quarter, but they controlled more money and things than territory or people. I went over all this with Elijah. He said that it might be a tough thing to get the elders to agree to, but they were practicable men and would go along as long as we did all the fighting and provisioning. They would be ostensibly neutral, and could even claim innocence, if for some reason we lost and were driven to the sea.

The plan was just to announce that we had been commanded by Allah to rule that portion of Medina not controlled by the Jews, and take over as a fait accompli. We would allow anyone to leave, if they wanted, but they could not stay unless they voluntarily submitted to Islam. There would be individual problems like aged parents of believers and marriages where only one member was an adherent, but those problems could be sorted out later, when we were in complete control. We did not plan on killing anyone if we did not have to, we just wanted to expel them from the region. They could take their property, but it would eventually come down to leave, convert, or die.

I did not foresee a huge problem. If we could successfully get the Jews neutralized, we would be way too strong for any organized resistance, and the only chance the enemies of Islam would have, would be to immediately fight. After conversions, voluntary emigration, and expulsions the other side would be weakened every day, as we grew stronger. I even got up a buying service to help unrepentant infidels to liquidate livestock, slaves, and other things. The plan was that the Jews and we would each contribute one-half of the capital to buy these things at 40-50% on the shekel. It was also agreed that no one else from either community would bid on any goods, and after things settled down we would split the profits.

Since I needed Elijah's assistance I decided to put the plan into action one month before his planned trip to Mecca where he was to marry Naomi.

The first camel we had to get into the caravan was the secret negotiations with the Jewish elders to divide the city, and split the profits this upheaval would bring.

CHAPTER TWENTY-THREE

The Crisis in My Belly

I was not the only one happy at this time; our entire community seemed to be enjoying the peace and prosperity of Medina. I guess the entire movement was unaware of just how much tension and pressure we were under while we were in Mecca. Getting out of that stinking anus of a town was the best thing that ever happened, and I had big plans to revisit the place of my birth with an entrance that would be remembered.

But fate continued to throw the gambling sticks. Destiny took a hand in a single action that brought forth emotions of both great joy and horror. I became with child. For an ambitious woman like me there is never a right time, but the thought of having Elijah's baby filled me with deep, deep love. I was ready, but there was just so much happening, and I really could not afford to slacken my pace in any way. I would just have to add one more task to my continuously growing schedule. But I was in a condition that filled me with love, hope, and expectations.

There was the immediate problem that I was an unmarried, technically revirginated, child of an exalted pretender.

Scandal would hurt the movement and me badly, so considerations and cautions had to be taken. I had become pregnant three times before in my whoring days, but the issue was immediately vaporized by abortives readily available and used at the brothel. My initial pregnancy came so fast after my disgusting, sick, rape that it might have been, horror upon horror, a product of my first coupling with my father. There are many times that I think I cannot believe how sane and focused I am, when you consider what a weird, truly ill upbringing I was subjected to. I was just hopeful that those abortions would not hinder my ability to carry to full term, and that I would be able to present a beautiful boy or girl to my beloved Elijah.

I obviously had to get married quickly, and to a fool I could easily manipulate. Hate him as I did, the irony was that the obvious choice, perhaps the only real practical choice, was my cousin Ali. In the best of all worlds, I would marry my baby's father, but this was Arabia and about as far from the best of all possible worlds as you can get. I gave myself one full day to think if there was any way to avoid the little, swishy sycophant, but it was hopeless, he was it. That day Mohammad had another divine revelation, the command had been given, I was to immediately marry my cousin Ali.

Now because of my beauty, brains, position, and access to wealth if I wanted anything, I did have suitors. Ali, on the other camel, was having way too much fun at the boys brothel to even think of marrying a woman. But I informed dad and then Ali and in three days we were officially linked in matrimonial rapture. Fast marriages were not at all uncommon at the time, and no one would dare count up to nine too obviously if they knew what was good for them. If the honeymoon baby was a little premature, it was not a real problem.

The wedding was a boring, ridiculous affair with many of the surviving members of my father's old crowd there. I wanted to be surrounded by those slovenly, drunken, puking imbeciles as much as I wanted to blow an elephant. It was the height of idiocy, to be surrounded by aged, filthy camelboys, just slightly and temporally cleaned up, to celebrate a sham marriage of a woman to a half of a man. I would no more want to really marry this fig packing finook, than marry a three-quarter ton camel.

Plus, the moron actually thought that he was obligated to try to screw me. Using every bit of control I could muster to keep from breaking out in tears of hysterical laughter, I listen as he explained his virginity with women, and his need for time to develop the desire that was necessary. When it got to the point of asking me to dress up as a young boy and to let him anally enter me, I could not continue. I had signaled him repetitively to just shut up for a couple of moments so I could control myself. My life had been extremely interesting to that point, but I had never been exposed to such extreme ridiculous humor. I have never been a person big with jokes, but I could have gotten the world to laugh at this pathetic joker. My husband, my husband the most miserable, pitiful wretched excuse of a man in the peninsula, wanting me to sashay my ass like a prepubescent boy so he could get it up. It was distressing, but the comic aspects were just too much. I could see the inner crisis that was tearing him apart, now that he thought that he would have to perform like a normal man. Tears we coming down both of our eyes, mine were in laughter, and his because he had never simultaneously displayed so many emotions of fear, disgust, and especially panic at the same time. For the first time in my life my sides were hurting in laughter watching this emotional wreck disintegrating in front of my eyes.

When we were securely in our honeymoon tent undisturbed by the rest of the world, I decided that I had to end the farce before this stomach fluttering humor would harm my baby. I had to be merciful with him, not because I wanted to but I had to end this giddy buffoonery. I explained to him that on this his wedding night, he could not sneak out to the boys brothel, but he had to stay with me; but to the relief of both of us, away from each other physically. I added that as the Prophet's and demigod Mohammad's daughter, I could magically get pregnant several times with his babies, because of our shared wedding kiss.

He was so relieved that he seemed to buy it camel, saddle, and harness. I had to kidnap him this one night so the faithful could fantasize about him depositing his seed in me. I explained that it was only because we were married that he was informed of the magic, and if he told anyone he would be immediately stuck down by Allah to die without the blessings of eventually joining Mohammad in paradise. I had gotten the idea from the Christian Bible about having a child without screwing. I was a revirginated woman who would have no sex with her husband, but I do not think that the Christian Joseph was quite such a swish.

CHAPTER TWENTY-FOUR

Planning the First Action

My life continued more or less in the same way. I managed to see the handsome Elijah in privacy almost every day and thoroughly enjoyed his skillful lovemaking, as we planned to take over Medina. I did have another confederate who was an immense help, friend, and confidant. My personal slave Shahrazad was a very intelligent girl, not all that pretty, but very loyal. We liked each other instantly, and she had been my personal slave since Ra'hel's death. Shahrazad was a few months older and her private life existence was dull and unfulfilling, but she lived an exciting life vicariously through me. I have always been more interested in men rather than women, but Shahrazad was definitely my best girlfriend, and I was hers. I needed and depended on her, and she was smart enough to understand her place and role, as my most important household woman.

Shahrazad knew to always outwardly practice Islam and

to respect the old fool publicly, but she totally understood the entire situation. As part of her duties, she kept an eye on Mohammad by supervision of his two slave girls who kept him as clean as possible. She also bribed the young slave boys so that they would be willingly buggered, and made sure that there was always booze available, if the drunk would slightly behave himself. She hungered for the love of a man, along with marriage and children, and she did have a few brief flings, but they always ended with many tears. I promised her that I would technically grant her freedom to celebrate the first birthday of my first child, or upon my 30th birthday, which ever came first, and also to secure a suitable husband for her, if she desired. I knew that was what she wanted, and upon freedom, she would become my salaried lady-in-waiting.

The slaves and servants had their own world within our world. Each side needed the other, but the situation was complicated and fraught with danger. There was no way we could exist without servants, but they could destroy us. The number one rule in Mohammad's household was that, under no circumstances, and this could not be emphasized enough, under no circumstances could Mohammad or Allah be portrayed in anything but the absolute best light. No jokes, snide remarks, tales, allusions, reports, news, or anything else would ever leave the household upon the pain of torture and death. This was non-negotiable and non-forgivable. A few times actions had to be taken, and examples made. Mohammad was revered and respected by the outside world; within the family compound he was dealt with as best we could.

.The servants all talked among themselves, and that was acceptable, they had to communicate to do their jobs. Shahrazad, who had a foot in each half of the household divide, was always listening and used her authority to protect my good name. I could not have carried on with Elijah without her assistance. She quashed any hint of a rumor of any of my actions, and kept me informed of everything happening at the compound.

I was forced to be nice and a little bit playful with my devoted husband when people were around. I would sit near him and even lightly touch and embrace him for practicality's sake. Thank Allah he was at least clean. He was even way too clean for a man, but then again he was not really a man.

As Elijah's wedding trip to Mecca approached, we were getting ready for the first power grab. Our negotiations with the Jews were difficult, but accords were reached and we came up with a secret date that we would make the announcement and fight to the death if need be.

We had an early graduation from both boy brothels. The lucky graduates were moved over to the constabulary. The few who were totally unfit for fighting were made eunuchs and kept on as slaves. This was an obvious incentive to the boys to develop their toughness, for it was graduation or castration. On graduation night, some of the girls from the various brothels were brought in, and the graduates could have their choice, girls or boys, or both for the whole drunken night. The next day they were rookie recruits in the constabulary, and subject to the pains and pleasures of a highly disciplined army. I always inwardly chuckled how when the boys matured, as they went from buggery to thuggery: truly it was a wonderful transition as we made money from them using their assholes to graduating and becoming very dangerous assholes. We did need each and every one of these perverted killing machines. They not only killed and maimed, but they struck fear within the very souls of the intended targets. If we had the strength to pull it off, we wanted this action to be a bloodless coup.

CHAPTER TWENTY-FIVE

The Battle for Medina

Everything was in place, and as the hour approached I was naturally very apprehensive. I loved being in this conspiracy with my beloved Elijah; we were moving beyond the physical love and deep mutual attraction to a strong emotional bond and partnership. Prior to this, I had been alone and I was so glad to be able to share the planning for the new expansion. Elijah was certainly a Jew, but I soon found out that he did not believe any of the sandy-schmandy religious nonsense any more than I did. I considered myself so lucky to have found a kindred soul who was sophisticated enough to see through the obvious crap that was spoon-fed to the populace. As we cuddled in cozy cushion talk, we often chuckled over imposing one more religion upon the yokels. Obviously the citizenry, slaves, and near everyone else thirsted for some magical, invisible make-believe, to allow them to make some sense out of their pitiful lives. They would be tithing and we would be spending; a fair exchange for us allowing them some elusive hope. We got even more than the gold, we received respect, honors, awe and fear. I loved the irony, that those people who did not have a clue about the real Mohammad, actually worshipped him, it would be akin to me worshipping a pile of sand flea infested camelshit.

However, it was not all smiles and giggles. If my plans fell flat, the devastation that would follow would be truly ugly. We did have many enemies and it might force me to suicide. If it meant being enslaved and reprostituted, with no hope of practical escape, I would prefer the nothingness of death, if I were not killed immediately. As a backup, if things turned to crap, and the long knives were coming out, I was going to flee to the Jewish quarter under Elijah's protection. There was no way my pusillanimous fig packed husband would escape the carnage alive. And 91 days after his death I could convert and marry Elijah in a legal Jewish ceremony. This might be enough to save myself, since I was nothing but a woman, and therefore of little importance.

We kept everything very quiet and on a need-to-know basis until the hour came. Elijah informed the Jewish leaders late in the night on the day before the take over. The constabulary was quietly called to the barracks one hour before midnight, and informed that they should get some sleep because they would be working in the morning. I actually managed to get a few hours of sleep that came in very handy later on that fateful day. In the morning I awoke Mohammad and sent his bedmate, a nine-year-old boy, back to the kitchen; I explained to him how he had commanded the takeover for today and all the details in a trance. He was somewhat hung over, but I explained the dangers and he had better just stay inside his sleeping quarters, until called to be joyously proclaimed the king by the town folk. Every semi-able bodied servant, adherent, and hanger-on was immediately conscripted into the constabulary. The squads had about 20 civilian soldiers joining three professional thugs. The squads were sent out to all the important crossroads, and one especially large squad was sent to the main town square.

Everything was done as noiselessly as possible and we had a special reception area set up by the woman servants next to our compound to welcome anyone who was smart enough to instantaneously convert. We had sweetmeats, drinks, and everything to make these people comfortable. We also planned to have the able bodied men, after they settled into Islam for a very short time, join the squads nearest their homes so their neighbors could see them and talk with them. The squad leaders were told that we wished to avoid any pitched battles, but it was almost preferable to kill one or two people if there was a more or less legitimate excuse and to make sure that the bodies were prominently displayed at the crossroads.

We tried to elongate the sleeping night and not awaken anybody. The word would spread, like sand in a windstorm, all by itself, and we were better off having the news reach different people at different times. When householders approached the squads, the squad leader or perhaps a Muslim neighbor told the person that Allah had declared

Medina the City of Allah, and that everyone must immediately convert to the true religion or leave. It was explained that the city was under martial law with a curfew, and males over eleven were restricted to their houses under pain of death unless they converted or were leaving the city under an escort. Those converting were embraced and brought to the welcome center next to the compound. Any adherent, who was inside a household that was mostly still sleeping, was embraced and told to go to the compound and await further instruction. Any converted slave who was owned by an infidel was freed.

A few really unintelligent men and a couple of nuts gave the squads some problems and were immediately killed. There were a couple of minor skirmishes that were quickly smashed. The one major confrontation concerned a dozen men from one extended family, who were upset over the killing of a crazed relative. They foolishly attacked the squad with disastrous results for them, all those men either died in the battle or were summarily executed. When the reports reached the compound, I took them privately into Mohammad as he was drinking his breakfast. I knew the family in question and they were hotheaded troublemakers; I then gave Mohammad's orders that the woman and children were to be seized, bound and taken to the main square and to be placed in the middle. I was told, and this was no surprise, that they were very visibly unhappy.

All in all, it was going more smoothly than I could have hoped. The new converts kept on coming in hour by hour.

Each family of converts that came was an encouragement for the remaining infidels to convert and almost two-thirds of the people converted by the final expulsions at the end of the week.

After twelve hours it was obvious that internal organized resistance within Medina would be absolutely futile. We had three men; all citizen conscripts, moderately wounded, one would eventually die, along with the battle death of one soldier. We also had two of our organized thugs separately executed by their squad leaders, for infractions while in action.

The new converts were told to go home and to enjoy their new glorious lives under Islam. We dismissed many of the citizen conscripts and rotated the rest as we did the men of the constabulary. A party atmosphere was encouraged, not a wild party, but a moderated good time. The grog shops and brothels were opened and well attended. With the family of hotheads, whose men had been killed in the ill-conceived battle, the younger members, both girls and boys, were brought into the various brothels and those who were sexually pure had their virginity auctioned off, while the younger wives were just unceremoniously added to the brothel staff. The older women, and two elderly men, who were too frail for the battle, and the very young children were told that they had three days to get out or be executed. Believe it or not, two days later, they very intelligently actually decided to convert. It was a masterstroke because Allah, in his infinite mercy, repatriated those unfortunate brothel inmates back into their family. Eventually they all gravitated individually to other separate families via marriages and though traumatized, they always praised the wisdom and mercy of Allah and his wise Prophet Mohammad.

CHAPTER TWENTY-SIX

Cleaning Up

There were of course problems but no disasters. A few diehards, who refused to convert or leave; had to be killed. We tried to dissuade them, but some people were too stubborn and too stupid to leave. I think a few were trying to make a brave point to an uncaring and deaf world. In any event, they ceased being a problem to us or anybody else. We confiscated the real estate of all the expellees, and bought their goods at nice prices. We also made sure that camel flesh was very expensive, so it was therefore very hard and dear to transport things out of Medina. All in all, we made a financial killing and the movement was now in control of three-quarters of Medina, and in alliance with the other quarter. The news raced through Arabia and the known world. It made Islam a topic of conversations and made more people both knowledgeable and curious. I was also sure that it deepened the hatred we had engendered within some segments of Arabia.

One thing that happened, I had not foreseen this at all, occurred during that hectic, near panic in Medina on the fateful first day, women who could go out and learn the news, soon found out that the Jews were unaffected. This in itself was no big deal, but about 150 people from several families went to the Jews and asked to be converted to Judaism. The Jews do not proselytize non-believers but allow sincere conversion. After some quick back and forth communications, it was agreed that they could take anybody they wanted if the Jews were satisfied that the prospective converts were sincere. From the point of view of Islam, these new converts were in effect neutralized as far as we were concerned, and being in alliance was definitely preferable to being our enemies.

The pace of camels over the sands is never fast. I knew if our enemies decided to attack it would not be quickly, so we had time to consolidate our power and make preparations if the attack did come.

We were suddenly pretty flush with money, Allah had commanded tithing, so money was coming in and would continue to do so. We moved the compound into much better quarters, which previously had belonged to families that had been expelled, and made preparations because there was a good chance that our enemies might try to dislodge us.

I decided to add more security to Medina by having a great trench dug around the city. Elijah had traveled to many other cities and had seen trenches and moats. A moat would be better, but it was impossible in such an arid place. It was a massive undertaking, but it did strengthen the defenses and the fact that we were building it let our enemies know that we were not going to be easy pickings. Obama was told to bring in a large amount of strong Nubian male slaves. It was back breaking work with a high mortality rate, but it was done and a large crew was permanently working to make sure that it was maintained against the wind and sand. Any army charging us would be severely slowed down and dissipated, while being subjected to volleys of arrows before reaching our walls.

In the meantime, Elijah traveled to Mecca to answer the prayers of Naomi who was finally going to shed her hated true virginity. I would certainly miss him while he was gone, and perhaps I was a little jealous of Naomi with her Elijah filled honeymoon. But I knew where his heart lay, and besides, in a way, I had a spouse too.

CHAPTER TWENTY-SEVEN

Mopping Up

Because we were new rulers, I had to be more lenient with infractions at the beginning. It would only be later that converting would be a one-way street, with apostasy resulting in death. At this early stage, if a family or individual wanted to leave the religion, it was permitted. There were not that many that wanted to leave, but I did not want to alienate the population any more than I had to. I was happy to allow the malcontents to leave and retain the smallest number of potential assassins in town as possible.

With Elijah gone off to Mecca to marry Naomi, I was afraid that there might be problems or misunderstandings with the Jews. Fortunately the events had led to good economic times for everybody. There was less bickering and I set up a caravan tax for anybody traveling in the neighborhood. The tax was not high enough to hurt commerce, but it was enough to bring in more revenue. It also kept the thugs busy patrolling the desert. We also had a lot of Muslims coming into Medina from other places and we were sending a lot of people out to proselytize. We had been very lucky that the first potential big battle was a walkover, but there were to be many more.

The takeover did disgruntle a very large group of angry people who dispersed throughout Arabia, even a few going beyond our peninsula. These displaced persons spread hatred and fear, but we were also sending pro-Islamic emissaries out to the world. The leading center of the Mohammad hating group, outside of his own compound, was in Mecca. This was not a surprise, and the heavy influx of refugees into Mecca vilifying Islam did not help the situation.

I knew that sooner or later, one city would have to conquer the other. There was too much bad blood and wealth to be plundered for the situation to remain static forever. I had been studying the methods of warfare for a long time, reading any scroll I could get my hands on, from Herodotus to Caesar, to learn the histories of battles and the art of warfare. In the coming Medina-Mecca conflict, it was obvious that one side should have the advantage. Whoever made the long, hot trek across the desert to the other city to attack, would be at the distinct disadvantage.

Merchants, relatives, and even caravan camel jockeys were always going back and forth, and we employed several trusted people to be in contact with specific spies who always kept their ears and eyes open. There was no way a major attack, troop movement, or armed call up could come without my knowing it in advance. Also, even if the Meccans could quickly and secretly put a large army together and somehow keep the information from me, it still would not work. Every caravan and loyal person who ventured out into the desert in any direction was under orders to immediately return or dispatch a fast rider straight back with information on any troop movements or anything unusual happening in the sand. A large army just could not make time like an individual rider. We always remained vigilant with lookouts, watchtowers and quick riders ready to be instantaneously dispatched; no one was going to sneak up on us.

I organized, trained, and provisioned the all Medina militia. Any male who could throw a spear was part of the militia, and I spent freely to make sure the equipment and training was top notch. Being a big believer in the value of women, I insisted that this large segment of society would not be wasted in wartime.

Various women and younger boys, not quite ready for the militia, were employed to back up both the regular soldiers and the militia with running the stores of extra equipment, food and water, medical attention, sending messages and tower lookout duty when every man was needed to fight.

I could decide if and when to attack Mecca, but the first necessity was to make Medina safe from an attack.

CHAPTER TWENTY-EIGHT

Motherhood

I found the caravan tax to be very lucrative. Most caravans just paid it, but others would avoid the Medina area, and attempt to circle around us and defeat the tax. This is where the glorious organized thugs showed their worth. These caravans were easy pickings for my killing machines. By being particularly brutal with two caravans early in the campaign, resistance melted. I divided the roving thugs into fairly small, about 15 to 18 sized, units and spread them from the Red Sea to the Persian Gulf bisecting the peninsula. Any movement from North to South, or South to North, had to pay or risk death, torture, and enslavement.

Because of the vast distances it was possible for a caravan to get lucky and make it through, but you could only be lucky so many times. It was far easier and cheaper to pay the five percent in money or goods at designated oases than to risk everything. I later raised the rate to one-fifteenth or 6.66%, after the tax and payments became well regulated, and paying the tax without complaint or evasion became the norm. We made a lot more by raiding and getting the goods, personnel and camels, but having people voluntarily coming to you and handing you money on a regular basis was a great thing, and in the long term very profitable.

Elijah and his bride Naomi came back from their wedding in Mecca, and I eagerly welcomed him back to my mat and conference tent. I was awaiting the birth of our first child and was again very happy. Elijah did tell me of the large anti-Mohammad fervor within Mecca, that he was even subject to possible assassination because of his association with Islam, however he was well protected inside the Jewish community by his powerful new father-in-law Aaron. It was still very important to keep our love relationship strictly quiet. Elijah said that the Jews of Mecca were very worried because they also foresaw the coming war and that it could have very dire consequences for them.

I was willing to play the defensive, waiting game as far as Mecca was concerned, because Islam was growing more powerful with both money and converts. We were now getting what I would call the turban holder converts. Our power was getting so great that some new adherents came to us because they figured that we would soon be the greatest force in Arabia, and they wanted to be on the winning side. The loyalty of these soft converts would always be suspect, but we needed everybody and every new person added to the psychological effect that Allah was the most powerful god. Many of the 'sunshine' Muslims would gravitate to be our functionaries, but they had to be monitored closely because these fair weather friends would desert us faster than a jackal's pounce, if a desert storm approached.

My birthing of our son Hasan was not difficult. Ali and I had all the normal ceremonies that a new son required. Hasan's real father was not there, and I did not want him there; I was afraid his pride and happiness might tip someone off to the real situation. When your husband is, as we say in Arabia, always flitting around like a sand flea, rumors of paternity must be kept in check. There were, thank Allah, several other half-men who were constantly banging boy's bottoms at the brothel, and they also had wives who regularly gave birth, so Ali was not the only new father who was a total swish. In private, Elijah could luxuriate in joy with his beautiful new son, who would hopefully grow up as a real man like his real dad.

Naomi quickly became pregnant and, believe it or not, it really did not bother me. Elijah was enough of a man to spread himself around a little, and I liked Naomi. I neither wanted nor could afford jealousy. To put it another way, I was as unlikely to be jealous of Naomi, as I would be of young Moostie, who was the eleven-year-old favorite of my husband Ali at the brothel. The only problem I had with the cute juvenile Moostie was that he had Ali completely wrapped around Moostie's little cock. When Ali decided that Moostie was to retire from servicing other men, I stepped in and immediately quashed that. Moostie's little ass remained available to every perverted camel boy who would raise six shekels. Moostie was on the effeminate side, not quite as much as his sugar daddy, but I wanted to make sure that he got toughened up a little and would not be castrated upon graduation, but would be sent to our army and hopefully killed in action while bringing greater glory to Allah. I definitely had plans for the pint sized junior pussyboy.

With the birth of our beautiful, strong son, no armies advancing on us, and our power growing in money, position, and converts, life was good. I had known a few girls lucky enough to be married to husbands that they actually loved; they were the exceptions, but they did exist. I knew of the joyful fulfillment that such a marriage could bring. I might have been legally married to a half-man, but my true marriage to Elijah, forever conceived in secret dread, brought me as much happiness as any girl in Arabia. I loved submitting myself to this wonderful Jew, I gasped in sexual delight as he worked me into fantastic climaxes, and I did not realize how much mother's love I could have for our son. Despite all the horrors, humiliations, and degradations I had suffered while growing up under Mohammad, the turnaround was so explosively great, that if my life had ended right there and then, I would not have felt cheated.

CHAPTER TWENTY-NINE

Caravans

Just about everybody in Arabia could see that a Medina-Mecca war was bound to happen. The two towns had been bitter rivals for generations, and had always approached life differently. Medina had much more rain and was able to grow some crops. The city started out as an agricultural center and market town. Mecca, on the other camel, was a caravan crossroad that had been developed by merchants and the related pimps and booze sellers who serviced the caravans.

The caravans were rough mobile entities, which made good money by bringing spices and other goods from places where they were cheaper to places where they commanded more gold. The desert is by nature very inhospitable and crossing one via caravan was not pleasant; the hours were long, arduous, and uncomfortable, subject to murderous raids by land pirates and the constant unmerciful heat. Caravans had been lost in the dunes, especially if stranded or disorientated by sand storms, and ugly deaths occurred whenever continuously circling camel trains ran out of food or precious water. Needless to say, the long trains employed tough, generally young, adventurous men who liked to party and celebrate the defeat of death whenever they reached a safe oasis. Mecca was a port town on many caravan routes, with a reputation for easy access to girls, boys, good food and especially booze.

When the camel jockeys reached the terminus or midway oasis, they received some pay and had a few days liberty to blow off steam, rest and re-hydrate. The namby-pamby types did not sign on or last if they did. Because of the nature of the difficulties, the caravan captain, and there was always just one, had life and death power over his underlings. Infractions such as theft, desertion, mutiny, or whatever were punishable by death or enslavement with no recourse to the offender. The danger of the trips was such that if one survived ten long trips you were lucky, very promotable to sergeant, and if you had been wise with your money, able to stake yourself to a business or buy land.

There was always danger when one caravan met another in the desert, especially if one was a lot bigger. If a battle erupted, one side or the other would be wiped out with no losers around to tell tales. When a huge long train would come in with just a very small contingent of healthy riders, and some goods that seem to be going the wrong way, everybody knew the story. Part of being a caravan camel jockey was to be a soldier, so the pay, being generally a share of the profits, had to be worthwhile or no one with any experience would sign on. Hiring slaves on caravans did not work out; they would often desert, with or without stolen goods or a camel, because such a slave had little to lose.

When the boys, with their oasis or trip money in hand, hit town there was no question of what they wanted to do. Two or three days later it was a whole different and quieter story. Three or four days after they had reach the town, they were generally much poorer and ready to continue the journey or sign on for the next trip.

If a caravan were heading south from the Levant, the captain ran the company, but a merchant or his representative was in charge of the cargo. When they reached Mecca, the merchants generally had two choices if the cargo had not been pre-sold in the Levant and was just being delivered somewhere. The cargo master could sell the contents in Mecca and then buy other stuff and head home, or he could after a small revitalizing rest, head farther south to Aden or another place. The cargo masters could deal with merchants tied to Mecca or swap with a northbound caravan and then they could both head home.

There were two places in Mecca for the cargo masters to meet. In the morning and midday there was a cool refreshment place, without any whores, run by a proprietor who made sure that his place was as breezy and comfortable as possible in a naturally good location. In the evening it was at the captain's room within the saloon & brothel formerly owned by Mohammad and now owned by the Dhinnah family. At each place there were interpreters, hired by the management, to facilitate trade talk.

Most of the caravans preferred to unload their goods in Mecca, and turn around heading home if possible. It was an old captain's tale that the further you went from home, the more chance there was for trouble. But, sometimes the long trains would travel great distances with the same cargo. The town of Mecca went out of its way to protect its livelihood by keeping the camels and cargo safe. The caravan trade was Mecca's dates and chickens, and safe caravans meant money. The camels and goods were watched, for cheap money, at the central municipal yards, and any thief or robber was publicly beheaded on Fridays or beforehand if the offended captain had to leave earlier.

The caravans were really like ships traveling the desert. The goods often went from being borne by camels to ships when the cargo reached the Mediterranean bound for Venice or Constantinople, or another seaport. Things did not move fast, but the movement of goods for hundreds, or even thousands, of miles brought money to everyone along the route.

CHAPTER THIRTY

Mecca's Opening Salvo

With my true love beside me just about everyday, coupled with my husband generally being away from my presence at the boys brothel, my baby Hasan growing strong and fat, along with the movement growing strong and fat too, life was going very well, obviously too well to last. Several reports came in on the situation that was brewing in Mecca. That ugly city was hurting economically because of our growing prestige and the caravan tax. Trade was the lifeblood of Mecca and we were putting the kibosh on it, as the number of caravans going through the town was diminishing.

The way the tax worked, when goods came into Medina the tax was extracted, but there was no fee when the same goods or, for that fact, any goods left Medina. You would pay one tax if you came from the south to the north and bypassed or stopped in Medina. You would pay one tax if you came from north to south whether you stopped at Medina or not. One tax would be paid if a merchant came to Medina and then sold it to another who moved the cargo out of the city. No matter how it was done, one tax, and only one tax, was paid, of one fifteenth of the cargo.

But something happened psychologically, it seemed, not in reality, but only seemed, like it was cheaper to trade in Medina. The human mind is odd and the perception is more powerful than the reality. Now, Medina was getting to be a major stopping place for caravans and a bigger trading venue. This engendered many things, as more traveling people came, saw the dynamic, safe city that was an Islamic City and therefore could see that we were not as others had portrayed us. The merchants, brothels and purveyors of spirituous refreshments were making good money from all the caravan trade. In fact, more people were moving in; if they were non-Muslim they had to convert, and then we got the religious tithe. The other major effect was that Mecca was livid. It is hard to describe the hatred in the reports that I received from our spies. A few Meccans were accused of spying for us and the mere accusation meant a horrible death. They caught a few of our real spies, but most of those tortured and killed were actually innocent. At that time in Mecca, if you had a real enemy the easiest way to neutralize him was to trump up a charge of being in league with Mohammad, and extreme ugliness would immediately come to that tent. This helped us because some Meccans figured this out, and it did not help with the patriotic unity a city needs in time of war.

All this great stuff was happening because of our camel bound constabulary of fierce psychotic thugs. They were the reason the caravan tax worked and the tax was the thing that was killing our rival town of Mecca.

The reports came in from our active spies; at this point, no one in Mecca was an acknowledged Muslim. Mohammad had even stated during a trance that when danger was apparent, it was not only allowed, it was encouraged to keep a person's Islamic faith secret. We had enough martyrs, what we needed were rich adherents and information. There was no question all the reports said the same thing that an all out war was coming our way.

In a way this was good because it meant that they would come to us, and in the desert it is easier to defend than to attack. Their first tactic was to defeat the tax by sending a huge, very well armed, caravan north bypassing us, and just going right through the area that we were control-ling. They would defiantly push through and be ready to defend themselves. It was kind of ironic, but it was so costly to put this all together and deploy the large number of guards that Mecca charged a ten percent tax to defend the monster caravan. The logic was that if they could defeat our less than seven percent tax, that it would be better for Mecca in the long run. As a practical matter it made little sense, but they were keeping us from getting our share of the goods.

We knew when they were starting out, but it was too risky to try to stop them. The point where they intended to breach our lines, which could change, was close to the Persian Gulf far from Medina, and we would have to risk our number one troops, the constabulary. Our killing machines were great, but the number of opponents was just too large. If our fanatics were wiped out then we would be almost defenseless. It was too impractical to conscript the citizenry and send them across the desert to wait for a battle where the enemy would control as to time and place. So the super caravan got through unmolested and the Meccans all celebrated, but it was a Pyrrhic victory because it cost so much to defend. In addition, the merchants were not all that happy because they arrived in the north, but all at the same time with largely the same goods so the prices dropped, too much supply with a limited demand.

As a taunt, the guards all went back to Mecca with a large south bound caravan, and they did it within seeing distance of Medina. We restrained ourselves to overlook this insult. War was looming but the important thing would be the final battle, not some minor skirmish or insult. The victor would be the one who rode the last standing camel.

The proof that their perceived victory was really worthless was that after the southbound caravan and the guards returned; no more mega caravans ever again left Mecca. Caravans did leave, but they paid their tax and went on their way. It was just too costly and impractical to run through our lines. They figured out that they had to try to kill the head of the snake. Mecca decided that they would have to defeat us in open warfare.

CHAPTER THIRTY-ONE

The Attack

It was only logical that Mecca had to attack us, and if they won they would regain supremacy. But this is Arabia, so it is not all cut and dried. After the caravans and guards returned to Mecca all kinds of internal strife broke out. One faction wanted to send out super large caravans with an army of guards every three or four months, while others highly ridiculed this proposal. Various families played the blame game because the super caravan just did not work. The merchants, who always were crying poormouth even during the best of times, loudly proclaimed that they all lost shekels or at best broke even. You could not expect to make much money if everybody was selling at the same place and time, and then everybody would be buying in the same place. Some of the super caravan merchants continued further north to be able to unload their goods away from the competition, but they all feared the return trip south. We in Medina gladly let them go south after imposing the caravan tax.

By our playing the waiting, defensive game, we had two advantages. The first was that the religious thing was still working, we continued getting more converts, and every convert meant more strength. Secondly, in the desert sands the defender always has the advantage. We could outwait them, thereby forcing the Meccans to make a move.

The logic was obvious to me: my chief advisor Elijah and the top military men I employed; we all agreed that the waiting game was the smart game. It took a lot longer for logic to take hold in Mecca. The tepid 'victory' of their super caravan brought out a lot of the old Meccan rivalries and infighting. They could bicker forever as far as I was concerned. Meanwhile, every caravan crossing Arabia, was depositing to us one-fifteenth of their goods or the equivalent in money.

Word finally reached us that after months of back stabbing, unhappiness and about a year after the super caravan, consensus had been reached and all parties within Mecca were united in the need to wipe us from the face of the earth. From that moment things moved much more quickly. This outcome of the future battle would mean the difference of prosperity versus ruin for them; so they put all their resources into the looming conflict. They amassed troops, camels, and mercenaries for the upcoming assault. It was literary life or death for me, and my son, because as a member of Mohammad's family through both birth and marriage, I would have little hope of surviving defeat. I would either be immediately killed or used as brothel fodder, as an insult to the prophet, for a month or two for all the common Meccan soldiers, and then publicly beheaded while the victors laughed and cheered. As a matter of practicality, I would take my own life and hopefully have my body somehow hidden or destroyed to avoid desecration.

This would be the first test of Islam. If we lost, everything would be gone, from the figurehead, to me, to all the top people. Even if Mohammadism somehow arose later; like the Phoenix from the ashes of complete annihilation, who would care. It would not profit me at all. Do you think I would give a mustard seed to have some false, fairytale memories of me continue through the generations?

So I prepared for the fight as if my happiness, life, son, and everything else were at stake, because it most certainly was. I whipped our morons into patriotic frenzy, after all Allah and his Prophet were being attacked. The obvious irony of this never seemed to reach anybody but the highly intelligent, which in Arabia means practically nobody. I can never get over the hopelessness of getting average people to understand the situation. I mean, if Allah in all of his glory really existed would he allow his drunken, perverted Prophet to be tortured and ingloriously killed? But we did manage to get the message out that we were all within Mohammad's big tent, and that death, torture and enslavement of everybody was at stake.

I purchased supplies, extra camels, mercenaries, and stockpiled food and life preserving water. I formed alliances with outlying tribes and renewed and strengthened our alliance with the Jewish quarter. The Jews were forced to throw their lot in with us because if we lost, nobody, Muslim or Jew, would be safe in Medina. I had the trench and city fortifications strengthened and had mandatory training for the militia. I saw that the women and older boys were not wasted but used as subordinates in many different ways. I encouraged and trained the elderly who could help, to have positions where they could assist. In short, I made sure that Medina was as strong as it could be, and that the fighting would be to the death. I also made military discipline very strict and had a few practical demonstrations of the necessity to follow orders without delay, without question, and especially without thought.

When all the reports form our spies and others started to pour in, I also became very worried. A torrent of sources simultaneously said that the army of attack was the biggest and toughest army ever assembled since Roman times. The next battle could be the last battle, one way or the other.

CHAPTER THIRTY-TWO

The Warrior Assets Himself

Fortunately we had great information, and we received reports on the huge Meccan army constantly. Since there would be rumors in any case, I had official progress reports put out daily. The populace was better off knowing the exact truth rather than panicking over false rumors. I forbade, under pain of beheading, any military age Muslim leaving the city without permission, and permission was not going to be granted to anyone. The elderly and disabled and some children were allowed to go to nearby places under the protection of some of our allies. Elijah would stay here with me, but he sent his pregnant wife Naomi to relatives in the North. I understand she carried on tremendously, but it was far better for everyone that she left with copious tears freely flowing. I would not leave my baby Hasan, I figured that I could not subject him to the tender mercies of defeat. It steeled my resolve to achieve victory or death.

Allowing for the time lag of getting information because of the distances the carriers and camel runners had to transverse, when the enemy was about one week from our fortifications, a huge problem appeared. A slightly more sober Mohammad decided he would actually personally command the troops. There was no question that this would lead to disaster, and he was very fearful but thought he was Allah's golden child and that he could lead the army to victory with Allah's help. He was on parchment the commanding general and Islam's absolute leader; and he was adamant about being in command of the city and troops.

I assigned eight quick-witted officers to him so that at least four would be flanking his sides at all times, to protect him and to keep him from publicly making a fool of himself. I had, up to now, been very successful at keeping him beyond the public's view. I suspected that his dumb wifelette, the still virginal Aisha, had her hand in this. She could see his loss of power within the household complex and wished to re-deify him for her own gain. Her father, another old camel breathed drunk, named Abu or Abe, he had a partially Jewish background, was very jealous of the household's wealth and power. It was pretty clear that Abe would like to see a young widow named Aisha control everything upon the Messenger's death.

The message to me was one of impending annihilation. The old fool, even with laying off the booze to some extent, was just too stupid and incompetent to run a fig and coconut stand, never mind an army. So he is talking and planning with all the generals, and beginning to again hit the grog harder, when he decides to launch a surprise attack on the Meccan army before they get to Medina. This is the desert, the odds of the attack being a surprise was about as likely as my husband's boytoy Moostie getting pregnant. And you can well imagine who was shaking in his sandals. I would have given even money that Ali would die in battle, from a fear induced heart attack. A regular soldier, only three times the man as Ali, would have been executed for cowardice on general principles, and I was married to this pusillanimous pansy.

The plan was for Mohammad, with Ali besides him, to ride out at the head of the army surrounded by their eight bodyguards, or babysitters. I had a special camel saddle made, at great expense, for Mohammad, a saddle that bound him into it, so he could not fall off no matter what.

Three days before the enemy was due, the long columns left Medina with ceremony and prayers, to go into the lion's mouth. Only a very thin guard of boys and old men were left to defend Medina. Actually, that was a bitter joke; Medina was totally defenseless, if more that 25 good, hostile soldiers showed up. We had three, possibly four, days before a victorious army would be marching in and it would probably be the Meccans, hell-bent to kill every man, woman, and child that they could find. It was not practical to run so Elijah, myself, and our little precious

Hasan waited in the eerie quiet of the probable doom. My one comfort was that I was more or less able to shack up with my true love and true husband, in heavy sexual togetherness, without as much fear of discovery within the quiet, panicked city.

The fog of war always produces uncertainties. The enemy knew exactly when our army, with its exalted general, left and they intelligently headed for a large low hill and dug in to obtain the high ground. All our planning and fortifications were going for naught and now Mecca was holding the defensive advantage. This meant a delay of another day or two before the victorious army would come marching in with blazing swords held high.

Our army reached the region in the afternoon, decided to camp out and wait until morning for the attack. In actuality they should have either dug in themselves and made the Meccans come to them or just rested, and at midnight, march back to the fortifications of Medina. We could more easily supply our troops, but logic did not rear its hoary head. In the morning, the glorious army of Allah, with all those men, young and middle-aged, formed to mount the attack, all of these maneuvers were easily observed; by the higher grounded army of Mecca.

In two pincer columns, both aiming for a frontal assault on the high ground, the flower of Islam moved at moderate speed. The enemy held back, and then, when the troops were very close to charging up the hill to victory or martyrdom, the enemy unfurled it barrage of metal tipped arrows. Thousands of archers rained havoc upon the conscripted infantry, as the singing sound of the missiles loudly and terrifyingly announced the incoming carnage. After the first volley, the archers fired at will as a constant hissing shower of death fell from the skies. The troops, at the cusp of the range of the arrows, mostly stopped and backed the columns up. No man, camel, or even a pup jackal could live long in that sustained fusillade of destruction. It was like a wall of metallic death falling from the heavens.

Mohammad and Ali watched in horror from the rear most command post, as the desert beneath our soldiers reddened to a crimson flood, which the sands quickly sucked up. A fast thinking major, on his own initiative, ordered the battle horns to blow retreat, trying to salvage as many lives as possible. Almost no one from the front or middle of the attack columns made it out alive. It was a complete and total rout. At the rear command post Mohammad and Ali could hear the faint cries of some of our dying men and the contrasting loud whoops and celebratory cheers from the Meccan forces. Ali, my brave husband, was forcibly restrained from running to his camel by two of his babysitters and Mohammad quickly quaffed dry several large drink pouches.

CHAPTER THIRTY-THREE

The Second Escape to Medina

With Mohammad getting rapidly and totally legless, I was told he was drinking as if he would never get another chance, and Ali being pinioned to thwart him from running blindly and madly into the desert, cooler heads had to step in and organize a rapid and orderly retreat to Medina. Our army, what was left of it, headed north as quickly as possible. The wounded that could be carried and looked like they might survive were transported out and those that had no hope of recovery were killed in an act of mercy. The crack constabulary, who had not yet been committed to the desert battle, brought up the rear to try to thwart any attacks.

The rapidly moving desperate army did not stop for 24 hours until it reached Medina in a state of total exhaustion and near panic. Wounded men, regular troops, camels, all dropped into any shade they could find. Our troops that were alive looked like their dead compatriots who were strewn out lifelessly in the hot dusty sand of the battle. This scene of our pathetic men lying half dead and looking helpless and hopeless was not a pleasant sight, and in sharp contrast to the proud men marching out of Medina only a very few days before. I made sure that all of the women ministered to the near dead soldiers; it kept their minds off their husbands, sons, brothers, and fathers who were not coming back.

I ordered that every camel have one boy assigned to cool, water, and feed if necessary. The boys were also told that they would be severely whipped if their camel died. The camels, with only one exception, recovered quite quickly, as is their nature, and in an act of clemency, I had this camel's boy only moderately caned.

The men took longer than the dumb beasts to recover both physically and emotionally; this was a major problem, as the Meccan army could appear at our gates at any moment. In our crisis, we had very limited intelligence because of the exigencies of the situation. But there was no way to rush the recovery short of the Meccan army being an hour away. Many men were exhausted to the point of sickness and needed time to stabilize. Mohammad and Ali were carried into the family compound. Mohammad had slept a large part of the way in total alcoholic stupor so he was not in that much distress. Ali was a different case, petrified with fear, coupled with exhaustion and panic, he was a total mess. When he was placed in a quiet, cool room and given water, he sank into the mats and pillows sobbing loudly for his little Moostie.

I stationed some older men a few miles from our unmanned trenches to scout for the approaching Meccan army. We were all but defenseless against the coming onslaught, and we dreaded that if they came soon we would have to send out a white flag of truce to see if we could get any surrender terms. Elijah and I resolved that we would take the last few fresh camels and hightail it out to the north with Shahrazad and our baby Hasan. I was not going to be captured alive in any circumstances.

Nightfall came and a few of the troops were beginning to look like they were returning to life. We rotated the scouts farther from the city on a few of the camels that looked strong enough to withstand the trip. The Meccans could attack in the relative coolness of the night, and I could foresee the savage scene with burning, looting, raping and death during a night of frenzied destruction and horror.

In personal exhaustion, Elijah and I threw caution to the winds, and secreted ourselves together for a possible last night of mutual intimate love. My confidant Shahrazad; again proved herself to be my most loyal, trusted, and valuable friend.

The Meccans did not come. When dawn arose over the Eastern desert, I left the family complex and saw that the men were mostly stirring and looked at least three-quarters recovered. We now had a partial defense; there would be no surrender. Our defenses might hold and every added hour that passed would help us immensely.

About two and a half hours after sunrise, one of our forward scouts came into sight with another rider. This was unusual because I knew this rider, he was a good, smart man, and he would not desert his post and ride into town without an excellent reason. When our man got close to the main gate he signaled and returned south back to his post as the other rider came in. The other rider was Idi, one of our covert adherents who had remained Mecca to spy for us.

I gave orders to have Idi taken to the complex and met him there. He had slipped away because he thought that his news was so important that he should break his cover. It was. The Meccan army, after some internal squabbling, had decided to return home in victory. I could not believe their stupidity. We could have been crushed into oblivion, we were totally spent, Allah would have been placed in the pantheon of ridiculed and useless gods. But this is what Idi reported and was almost certainly true.

I put word out that the next day would be a day of celebration, remembrance, and praise to Mohammad and Allah. I sent six riders, young men who had recovered from the battle and retreat, south to confirm the story of the Meccan army returning home. After sending out additional scouts to the North, East, and West to insure that the possible invaders were not flanking us with a coming attack, I marveled at our luck and prepared for the coming day.

We were in the jaws of death and escaped; thank Allah that the Meccans were fools.

CHAPTER THIRTY-FOUR

All Praise to Mohammad

Even though our six riders had not yet returned, we received other reports all confirming that the Meccan army was going south. In theory, they could reach Mecca, rest for a few days and then come back to attack, but that was not very likely. Despite the foolish tactics that were employed by our side, we had, through their stupidity, survived, and with our survival, anything could happen. It turned out that we lost about 30% of our army killed, with just a few soldiers maimed to the point of being unable to ever fight again. Just about all of our dead were of the conscripted infantry, who were the most expendable. Our crack, organized thugs did not lose a man, but did observe the din and fury of battle: this was probably a small plus.

We were down but far from out, and it was the time to put the best possible spin on the events. A day of celebration, remembrances, and praise to Mohammad was quickly organized. This became a mandatory event for everybody, to honor the families who had lost members in the battle. The few wounded men who had died after reaching Medina were solemnly buried with great dignity and honor. The funeral ovations were long and glorious with musicians contributing requiems and dirges. It was made plain that this funeral was not only for the few men actually being buried that day, but, symbolically, for all the fallen heroes and martyrs, whose bodies were left in the sands of battle.

Each and every fallen man was already in paradise enjoying a lifestyle that could only be dreamed of on earth. Long descriptions of how wonderful it was to be allowed into the special paradise of heaven for those lucky enough to have fallen in battle, while serving Allah, were emoted with tears and deep passion. How these earth-bound orators knew all these things was not brought up.

Later, after the feasting and much public drinking, another round of oratory commenced to praise Mohammad, the Servant of Allah, who guided our troops both into battle and back home in victory after stopping the Meccan hoard, and forced them back to Mecca in fear. It was the genius of Mohammad, who was aided by divine inspiration, and the brilliant counsel of his general and heir, Ali, to get Mecca to exhaust all of its energy in futilely attacking, until the army was spent and totally vulnerable to being wiped out by our counter attack.

Only the villain and traitor, the spy who ordered the retreat to be sounded just as total and absolute victory was to be achieved, had cost the army of Allah complete annihilation of the enemy. The fact that the wounded and exhausted army of Mecca was able to drag itself back to their fortress of Mecca was deplorable, but they had been beaten and humiliated and would soon probably sue for peace. It was only treachery that allowed the enemy to limp back wounded and in disarray. Mohammad be praised, Mohammad be praised, Mohammad be praised.

The final speaker did not speak at all. A cleaned up, reasonably sober and somewhat somber Mohammad, who was still grieving those many brave fallen friends, approached the speakers podium, but was drowned out of any possible words by the gigantic yelping and screaming of the delirious crowd praising his name. The joy, love, respect and vociferous admiration continued for minutes until the prophet waived in acknowledgement and left, surrounded by a cacophony of love.

As a final culmination to the assembled masses, the major who had turned out to have been a spy and traitor, who had snatched assured victory by having the retreat horns blown, was brought up to the speaker's dais bound, hobbled and gagged. The crowd yelled louder than any Roman crowd at any gladiatorial game or gory spectacle. The mob was hushed after several moments, by the master of execution, who explained how this evil traitor had been responsible for so many deaths and allowed the enemy to escape certain total destruction. It was added that he had secreted himself as a jackal in the flock, as a sheep wearing woolen clothing, all while professing total piety to Allah. He had deceived everybody, his family, his wife, her family, everybody but Mohammad, who had suspected that something was amiss. The traitor alone would be punished, but his family, who happened to be powerful, was to be absolved of all vicarious sins.

The condemned traitor was placed in front of the crowd and made to prostrate himself as a powerful executioner, with one mighty swoop, beheaded the turncoat to the wild, blood-happy cheers of the throng, and raised his severed head high to a long thunderous, frantic ovation. An announcement was then made that all the grog shops and brothels, ordered closed as a mark of respect to the honored dead, were now open and everything was free on a first come, first serve basis. It was truly a night that the early adherents of Islam long and lovingly remembered.

CHAPTER THIRTY-FIVE

The Recovery

The day after the celebration was an unofficial holiday of recovery. With the hurly-burly of the last week finally subsiding, the reality of the many deaths sank in to the families of the fallen. Not one resident of Medina, had not known at least a score of missing men who would never be coming back. I had to get started to quickly and efficiently rebuild our strength.

Arabia rapidly returned to the normalcy of pre-war trade and the caravan tax was still being imposed with the shekels coming in, like mother's milk, to our coffers. Runners were sent out to all our compatriots in the various cities and towns to inform them of the true account of Mohammad's brilliant victory, and to command that all single men between 19 and 50 were to relocate to Mecca within the next four months.

As we were rebuilding our strength, the fools in Mecca continued to squabble among themselves. The smarter ones could see that we were continuously getting stronger; they had blown a gigantic opportunity to wipe us out. The other side thought that victory had been achieved with their army only losing one soldier, in a freak accident, during the one-sided battle. They figured that Islam was crippled beyond recovery, and that their position as the local hub would remain strong.

Our spies and other sources all reported that it looked as if no army would be forming to attack us, at least not in the foreseeable future. This was exactly what I had hoped to hear. Our movement needed the time to regroup and re-flourish and time was, again, on our side. The constabulary went back to their pre-battle line across the peninsula to insure the collection of the caravan tax, and the converts were still signing up. In a very short time, we were up to our battle day strength and I had a long talk with dear old Dad reminding him that he had almost ruined everything, and that he must leave all things directly with Allah, who would communicate with him through the trances. The Prophet had seen his miserable life flash before him on that fateful day of the infantry's slaughter, and he personally was not ready to die. He promised me that he would always, from this point on, await instructions from Allah on all matters. Along with everybody else, old Mohammad himself was clueless as to who was running the show. I still shook my head over the fact that these people were so easily fooled. The word had come down from Allah through me, and they obeyed. After all, Allah was telling them what to do, and Allah held the keys to heaven and eternal salvation.

CHAPTER THIRTY-SIX

The Affair of the Necklace

My life was very busy. I was coordinating the rebuilding of the movement's strength after the self-inflicted disastrous defeat. I had some of the Prophet's revelations refer to the 'battle of the trench', because I wanted to confuse everything about the defeat and by mis-naming and relocating the battle it would be easier to lie and reverse the true facts on our heroic victorious defeat. When the word is coming down from Allah, people will believe the spin rather than their own eyes. I could hardly believe it myself, but the way it works, the morons will not only believe the spin, but they will fight anyone who remembers the truth.

I also had the ever-present difficult task of keeping all talk and rumors about my love life with Elijah quiet, and squashing any discussion about the behavior of the old drunk. To add to my problems, my little teenybopper step-mom Aisha was beginning to sexually awaken. So this mirror-loving little drama queen is looking with fascination at each and every good-looking guy floating around the complex. She is batting her eyes, twitching her butt, and breathing heavily while raising her rib cage whenever any cute guy is within sight. This emerging little bitch jackal is laying it out there for all comers. She was even doing her 'come hither and let's see what happens' routine in front of my man Elijah. The fact that he was married to Naomi did not seem to slow her down or bother her a bit. The little virgin seemed desperate to change her status; not with her crusty camel breathed husband, but with some young, hot meat. The cutesy pie little flirt was developing into an attractive woman, but her behavior was bordering on the scandalous. I had to talk to her about toning it down as a wife of the Prophet of Allah. When I got to the part about whipping and beheading, I think it, at least temporarily, sunk in. It was so ironic, here the alcoholic perverted fool could screw all his pre-pubescent daughters, but his legal wife was a long time virgin. She had him so wrapped around her pinky it was disgusting. Lately, when he was not buggering any of the boys, she was throwing a sexy young Nubian slave girl named Maria his way. Aisha did not care who, or in his case, what Mohammad screwed, as long as it was not her unsullied virginal body that was getting the honor. She was saving herself, for anybody else. I hated the little egotistical bitch, but had to tolerate her.

Aisha had a cousin, on her mother's side, who was one of the few people she got along with. This cousin, who was Aisha's age, had just gotten married and moved to her husband's town about 5 days away via caravan. I had met the bride briefly, and needless to say, she was another self-centered, lazy gimme girl, absorbed with her looks, clothes, and jewelry. Well, one of Aisha pampered cats had just had a litter, and it then became imperative that she had to personally give her cousin a calico kitten as a wedding present. Getting permission from her old fool of a husband was easy for her, but I could easily figure out this story. She wanted to be out of sight and out of mind to meet some stud, at this point probably any stud. This vixen was in heat and wanted to get laid, waylaid, parlayed, and marmalade; it was retching.

Naturally I insisted that her beloved husband accompany her to Aisha's great disappointment. She wrangled for Maria to come along, as well as, a young cherubic slave boy, so Mohammad would not be bothering her with any carnal desires.

On the third day after they set out, Aisha came up missing. Everyone thought she was on the caravan, but a thorough search proved futile and it was decided to send Yusef, a tall and tough young officer, back to the uninhabited oasis where the caravan had overnighted. The caravan was three to four hours away from that oasis, so Mohammad thought that the entire company should press on to the next scheduled stop; Yusef would see what was up and meet the train later.

Who shows up a day and half later, at midnight, but

Yusef and Aisha atop the same camel. She had this long, involved camelshit story about losing her wedding necklace, the one she had extorted as a wedding gift from the old drunk, and searching for, and finding it, and being abandoned by the caravan, and thank Allah, Yusef came back to save her. But she was fine now and from what I understand, was even, for some reason, wildly happy.

CHAPTER THIRTY-SEVEN

The Necklace Aftermath

Well, comparing the old, smelly Mohammad to the strong, handsome, well built Yusef was like contrasting a pristine, beautiful oasis with an old flea infested camel turd. When everyone returned a couple of weeks later, it was not hard to figure out who got stuffed, and who did the stuffing. If it were not for the rumors and impending scandal, I would not have really cared, but this was the royal family, at this point, and Mohammad could not be publicly cuckolded; by a flirtatious little teenage airhead in heat.

The little bitch also confirmed the fact that Yusef had gotten her cherry by her terrified actions. She must have feared that the strong young stud had impregnated her, and that old camelstink would remember that he had never actually screwed the little lynx. So, biting the camel's ass, she romanced the ancient fool, got him bathed and fumigated, and actually, in an act of desperate total whoredom, had sex with him, twice. I can imagine her revulsion and horror. It still brings me to tears of pleasure and non-stop laughter to imagine the absolute internal disgust and retching abomination little miss precious had to go through to excite and service old camelfart. What desperation and being scared shitless will do! I adore reflecting upon Aisha's worse nightmare of having the decrepit, filthy, flatulent, fool slobbering all over her, and then carnally entering her precious body. Whenever I need a good laugh I think of that horrified and panicked little adulterous whore, who now had a much better understanding of life at the bottom end of a brothel.

The problem was that the busybodies were spreading the rumors almost as fast as Aisha had been spreading her legs, and action had to be taken. I had the name of a guy who was actually blaspheming Allah with this adultery story and had him arrested and confined out of town. This put a damper to any open talk, but it did not stop the whispering.

Mohammad had a trance and Allah come forth with words of wisdom. Allah said directly that Aisha had never strayed from her beloved husband, but that false claims of adulterous behavior were to be punished. Allah further commanded that any claim of adultery had to be testified to by no less than four male eyewitnesses. Now, there were times when I was brothel fodder, that twenty waiting guys would see me blowing a succession of camel jockeys, but outside of brothel work, sex is usual pretty private. In Aisha's case, when she was being gloriously jumped, lumped, rumped, and pumped by Yusef, nobody was around, so the four eyewitnesses rule was impossible to get around, unless she confessed, and that was unlikely because she preferred having her head attached.

The loudmouthed jerk I had arrested was terribly sorry for his foolishly repeating a rumor he had, at this point, absolutely no faith in and apologized profusely. I let him off with a public whipping.

I also added an interesting Koranic law via revelation. Allah said that no wife of his Prophet could ever remarry under any circumstances, under pain of beheading. I knew that that would fix her caravan, and keep her from getting pregnant after Allah finally took his alcoholic conduit to his reward in paradise.

She never did get pregnant, or if she did, no little bastard ever survived long enough to puff out her belly.

CHAPTER THIRTY-EIGHT

The Scoundrel Chaim

It seemed almost certain that a final battle with Mecca was looming, but time was on our side, so I did not push it. We were investing quite a bit of time, shekels, and effort into diplomacy. The more friends we could assemble by cajoling, bribing, or bullying, the better off we were, of course, Mecca was trying to do the same thing. When the intercity battle would come, any troops from some neighboring town or oasis shooting arrows with us, was far better than shooting them at us.

Elijah was helping me with the diplomatic end and we happily became pregnant with our second child. When I was four months gone, I informed my sweet husband of the impending birth of 'his' child, and the childlike fool was actually happy. He gladly echoed the word about the Prophet's seed being again propagated to all his fellow perverts at the boys brothel, and they were all deliriously happy and proud. The only exception was Ali's little favorite Moostie, who had not figured out the story. The insignificant little fag should have realized that Ali only had so much sperm, and it was all going Moostie's way.

Naomi, Elijah's wife, was also preggers, and that did not bother me a bit. We had to keep up appearances at both ends, and this magnificent Jew was man enough to carry it off with no problems. It is hard to believe this ridiculous world of ours, where I am married to this sissy, who could not get it up with a woman if his miserable life depended on it, while my soul was intertwined with the love of my life, who was one thousand times the man my husband was. The irony was also enhanced because no one could know; Allah certainly worked in mysterious ways.

On the diplomatic front we were making good progress with our treaties and alliances, but we ran into one particularly sticky problem. Most of the various Jewish tribes, sub-tribes, and factions were led by men like Naomi's father, Aaron the Wise, intelligent, well read men who were reasonable and trustworthy. They may drive a hard bargain, but once they were bought, they stayed bought.

In one particular tribe a low born, uneducated, but street smart, scoundrel had clawed his way to leadership. This fellow known as Chaim was famous for his double dealing and treachery. After we had made a solid agreement with him, which cost us plenty, we received absolute proof that he was negotiating with Mecca and giving all types of information on us. Elijah was furious and just wanted to wipe the tribe out as an example, but we took the bad situation and did the best we could with it.

We fed Chaim some misinformation, which rapidly rebounded to us via Mecca. We entrapped and quickly captured his entire tribe with only a few exceptions. The fate of Chaim was sealed; he had to be made a public example. He was going to be one more sheep brought to slaughter, so that all the other sheep would see the folly of treachery against Islam. We quietly let one half dozen small families 'escape' after they recovered and delivered all the treasure that the tribe had accumulated. We then offered, as an alternative to beheading, the male family leaders a deal, convert to Islam and be welcomed to a new brotherhood and to live in peace with their families. Only a few of these morons accepted. These other men, many of whom seemed intelligent, went to their deaths, with their families placed into slavery, in alliance to some invisible illusion. I thought, what is the difference between our brand of camelshit and their brand? Many people would praise their solid steadfastness, but I just thought that they were fools. It reinforced, to me, the notion of just how powerful this paradise-Allah thing, we were selling, was. Death and dishonor versus worshipping something that did not exist, not a hard choice for me.

After the beheadings, Chaim was the last to die, and was not pardoned on his pleas that he wanting to convert; the slaves were sold, our treasury enriched and most importantly, fear was put into the hearts of all the other tribes of Arabia.

To many people, getting with the program and praising the old drunk was beginning to look like the best and safest way to survive in times that tried men's souls. The whole peninsula was being forced to choose, you were either for us or against us, and we had a lot of sweetmeats and we had a lot of steel.

CHAPTER THIRTY-NINE

The Growth of the Koran

I decided to add to the Koran parts that glorified Mecca and Mecca's role as a holy and essential city. I wanted to build up the war fever to take back Mecca from the infidels. We were going not on a military adventure, but a crusade to rescue the holy city from the unbelievers.

I was always revising the Koran but now I was doing a more wholesale job and putting in how everyone must visit the holy, sacred birthplace of both the religion and the slovenly drunken figurehead. I added the need to partake in rituals and I liked the spectacle which the half naked boy whores had of walking around the old rock counter clockwise seven times to excite the old perverts. I legitimatized that to make it an obeyance honoring Allah. It was an inward private joke, I would have the faithful men parading around like they were boy whores sashaying their asses to entice perverted men toward buggery. It was so ridiculous and laughable, I just loved the thought of it. The comic aspect of the whole thing just perversely warmed my heart and funny bone.

I also had to clean up certain passages that upon

reflection brought out the true nature of the revered Messenger. I pondered a bit, so I could get the precise wording I wanted. It was difficult to insert exactly what I needed, but still have it so I could easily change words, themes, or passages. I did not want passages so eloquent and striking that they would be easily quoted or remembered and therefore hard to alter.

There were plenty of eunuchs around and they were obviously wifeless and childless. They were almost all like old never married women, full of complaints, dislikes, and grudges. They seldom fought like men, but were catty and backbiting. These eunuchs were the perfect guardians of the Koran.

I set up a system where there were three chief masters of the Koran with three sub-masters and a bunch of younger eunuchs in training. The three masters were the absolute authority on the holy words and upon death a sub-master would be promoted and a student would become a sub-master. It was possible for a sub-master to be demoted, but the only way out for a master was death.

None of the masters, sub-masters or students was literate or allowed to learn how to read. I put forth the rational that they must know the Koran by heart, without the crutch of parchment. I kept the written records myself, and when I wanted to change something that was already Koranic, I asked the masters a question. They would recite the Koran, and I would then inform them that a mistake had been made, produce the parchment that they could not read, and have them correctly learn the new revised passage. There was a bit of doublethink involved, but after a few beheadings because of forgetfulness, I found three eunuchs who were very compliant and happy to live their comfortable lives. They all hated each other, acted like horrible old maids and were just unpleasant to be with, but they mouthed the correct words with authority and made sure the sub-masters and students got the new passages right.

Some unfortunate things had sneaked in the Koran that had to be rectified, including any reference that could hold dear old dad in an unfavorable light. I made sure that only the trance words from Allah were included, and not any words that were merely personal and not for the universal good of mankind. There had been a few parts that had to be altered such as "After the Prophet Mohammad spoke about the prayers to be given at the funeral of a mother-in-law, he said 'I think I have to barf.'" About two or three times a week, fluctuating on how badly he was drinking, he would utter his well known warning "I think I have to barf." And within a second or perhaps before the words were fully spoken servants, family members, frequent guests, and everybody else in the household ran away in an outwardly circular pattern, because the prophet would then projectilely puke in whatever direction he happened to be pointed to, as if he were a fountain of vomit. If you did not hear the magic words, but observed the mass circular fleeing, you would without thinking join the exodus.

The puke was bad enough, but the smell would gag a camel or a herd of elephants. An entire tent would have to be evacuated until the lowest ranking slaves had cleaned it up and aired the tent out, while beginning the process of freshening up the Messenger of Allah.

CHAPTER FORTY

War Preparations

Although we could not publicly connect the dual celebrations, both Naomi and I delivered Elijah's sons on the same day. It was the second child for each and I had, in little Hussein, another beautiful strong boy who would hopefully grow up to be like his magnificent father. Even my sissy husband was flitting around in the joyous news and the old drunk was glad to add another grandson.

I was busy in the necessary planning for the Meccan war. We were having success lining up allies and troops for our cause and thwarting Mecca's efforts as often as possible.

I began by starting skirmishes with any tribe or group that favored Mecca. They were skirmishes for us, but they were life or death for our enemies. I cut a broad arc of territory to the Persian Gulf and moved the organized thugs to this arc of land to enforce the collection of the caravan tax. By making sure that every town, oasis, and tribe were our allies to the north of this arc, we closed most of the anti-tax smuggling activity. I reinforced our small navy on the Red Sea to stop any evasion of the tax by boats and had my old ally Obama extend the line into the African side of the Red Sea. We had a very secure line that was not going to be crossed without our share of the goods given to us.

The line in the sand also isolated any pro-Mecca factions north of the line from assistance from Mecca. These stranded areas were soon won over without the need to fight. They did not have a chance and were not suicidal, so they all sued for peace and alliance. I greatly preferred live friends than dead enemies, and our empire kept growing.

Our next goal was to subdue Mecca and get control of the entire Arabian peninsula; from there we could expand in any or all directions. The key was the destruction of Mecca. I had the sheep-like populace chanting the new slogan at all public rallies and gatherings, " Mecca must be destroyed." "Mecca must be destroyed."

I also used my old paid up screw buddy Obama, in a delicate family matter. We had gotten the little bitch Aisha's case settled down scandalwise, but she could not let well enough alone. All of a sudden, who was around a lot more often, but her cherry popping stud Yusef, and the dumb little bunny was all of a sudden much more quiet, friendly, and complacent. As if this camelshit was going to get by me. She also managed to disappear for short durations while Yusef was in the immediate vicinity. Although I would have liked to have an excuse to separate her from her head, I had to think of the scandal and controlled my instincts. In any event, I had to move quickly before her actions became common knowledge.

Obama was heading back to Africa, so Yusef was assigned to him as his liaison/bodyguard. Obama and his officer figured to be gone for somewhere in the vicinity of six months, give or take. I explained to Obama that nothing was to happen for at least four months or so, unless he had to quickly return to Medina for some reason, but that under no circumstances was Yusef to ever re-cross the Red Sea back to Arabia. It seemed that while in Zanzibar, on a slave buying trip, Yusef got sick from some deadly African disease and quickly succumbed. Aisha's loverboy was honorably buried with a dignified ceremony; at low tide in a shallow grave next to a crocodile swamp, and he very quickly disappeared from history.

Needing to let things play out a little and hoping that my desire for comic relief would be well rewarded, I bided my time with Aisha. She came through and gladdened my heart and funny bone, for Mohammad again got lucky with her. The emotional ups and downs this little she-jackal must have gone through. She had enjoyed her fling with Yusef, and now had to pay the heavy price with Mohammad.

I surmised that she would actually like to become a mother and have a real live play doll, but sleeping with the old malodorous drunk was not worth the price. But if her great big strong stud had knocked her up, that would have been fine, except that old camelstink might catch on that he could not possibly be the father because of inactivity. So again, fearful of her life if she came up with a big belly, she cozied herself up to this pathetic, cursed man that she could neither stand or smell, and allowed herself to be emotionally and physically raped. They truly deserved each other. It was a story of her horror, his fulfilled lust, and my schadenfreude. At this stage of the game for old Mohammad, I can easily and joyfully imagine what she had to perform to get a rise out of him. I cannot believe how much pleasure I received mentally reviewing the two, count them two, sessions she put in, insuring her head.

While this was all going on, our spies in Mecca were all bringing in good news. Fractionalism had broken out in the city and the various sides were at each other's throats. There was no internecine bloodshed yet, but they were infighting for control of the city. I knew that this was the time to take advantage, while the sands were burning hot.

I gathered a new, powerful army with our troops, citizen soldiers, allies, and mercenaries. I paid through the camel's ass for the mercenaries, but I wanted Mecca to have none left to purchase. We amalgamated the largest army the world had seen since the Caesars ruled Rome, and we could feel the invincibility as it all came gloriously together.

With the aging Mohammad nominally in charge, my pixie husband at his side, the real generals were ready to clash in war, to destroy Mecca in an absolute triumph for Islam. I could not see how Mecca could withstand the onslaught of this largest of armies with mounted camels, archers, and a huge number of infantry. There was no sense sparing any expense, it would be victory with immense power and wealth or perhaps defeat, destruction and death.

All the segments of the Army of Allah were well equipped. We had spare provisions of every type, and even medical care. We would not run out of water, food, bows, arrows, axes, spears, camels, or shields. Discipline was severe and at every dawn, at least two problem children were publicly executed for some infraction, be it desertion, theft, spying, sedition, or insubordination. This was a well regulated killing force, eager to reclaim from the infidels, the birth city of the Prophet, and the Prophet reported that Allah promised a total, magnificent triumph, and death to all who oppose the all powerful Allah.

CHAPTER FORTY-ONE

Marching Toward Armageddon

The weather was pleasant, as I sashayed atop my camel, encircled by my smartly attired bodyguards I ebbed and flowed like a dancer to the soothing beat of the horns and drums of the boy's battle corps, almost oblivious to the other dull sounds of camels and men, while observing the all encompassing panoramic yellow sands interspersed with moving displays of bright and various colors. With this heady and auspicious pageantry we ceremoniously began the epic journey, one which would achieve triumph or death, as I moved headlong toward the most important day of my life.

We had our huge army and Mecca seemed to be in disarray. We had learned their lesson of cheap declared victory and meaningless triumph. Success meant smashing these infidels to total prostrated submission or death. The upcoming battle would not be a draw; it was victory or total defeat.

I had to be there to observe the action; this was the biggest day for Islam, hence the biggest day for me. I was in charge of the women's brigade to assist with messages, supplies, medical assistance, and military observations. I do not and did not believe in fate, but if my life were to be over, I would go down with a knife in my hand, either as an aggressive weapon or an implement of suicide.

My lover and soul mate, Elijah was a captain in one of the Jewish brigades, and our sons were temporarily safe with my devoted Shahrazad back in Medina. I carried the heavy knowledge that the future of our sons hung in the balances as well. All the sacrifices, the pains, the triumphs, deceptions, planning and horror were aimed toward this Armageddon. I, in the name of Allah, would win or the movement, like scores of others in previous times, would fizzle to obscurity.

For reasons of logistics and safety, we took a slightly circuitous route going through the Red Sea fishing village of Jeddah. Our provisioning teams were sent out nine days before the Army to the various stops where we would encamp along the trail. There was no way in Hell that our massive army's movements would be a surprise to Mecca. It would be their choice to meet us in battle along the way, in front of the city, or to defend the city walls. We figured that they would probably choose to fortify and defend the city itself, but that was their choice and in a sense it did not matter. We were going to fight them to the death somewhere and the place was, to an extent, secondary. It also became much more difficult to get communications from our sources inside the city.

We planned a journey of about twenty days duration to reach an elevated plain near Mecca. We could camp there for the final preparations, if we could reach it before being engaged in battle. We headed southwest toward the Red Sea, crossing the Tropic of Cancer and eventually reaching Jeddah for a three day rest. Time was not as important as keeping the army intact. Mecca was not going anywhere and conserving our strength was the paramount issue. Along the way we even recruited several hundred new recruits, who were mostly older teenage boys thinking only of glory and too stupid to realize the realities of war and death. A few of the new recruits had second thoughts and tried to desert to their homes. It had a sobering effect, when those who were caught were executed in front of the other new recruits. Death to deserters with no visions of the paradise and virgin camelshit, that we fed these overly hormonal saplings, the sex came only after honorable death in battle, fighting for the grand illusion.

Mecca, probably wisely, was busy fortifying the city, desperately pulling in allies, and trying to achieve unity before the onslaught. We reach the heights in good order, and with the absolutely largest army ever assembled in the memory of any living person.

We warily rested for a day and a half after the last contingents reached our base. We did the final preparations for the assault and tried to bring the troops and support people to a fever pitch about retaking the sacred city from the infidels for the greater glory of Allah and his Messenger, who happened to be hidden away in an outside tent totally inebriated.

CHAPTER FORTY-TWO

The Cake Walk

While we bivouacked right outside of Mecca, some exciting and interesting things were happening. Both sides had scouting parties observing the enemy, and a few small skirmishes would break out if the squads got too close to each other. We also received into our ranks some deserters who came individually and some that were sent with messages from inside the Meccan walls. Surprisingly we observed a white flag of truce by a small camel riding contingent that we allowed near our base under the normal rules of conflict. Doubly surprising, as far as we could tell, we had not lost one man to the enemy by desertion. You always expect a few, out of the many thousands, to flee to the enemy for one reason or another, but here logic was keeping everything intact. Our forces appeared unbeatable and it would be doubly suicidal to attempt to cross to the enemy lines, because it would be death if caught, and death if one were successful, but then we won the battle. I was feeling much better and more confident, and that confidence factor frightened me a tiny bit.

The reports from inside the city that we received all

said the same thing, which meant that it was very probably true. Mecca was in chaos. The factions were almost ready to declare war on each other inside the city. Defeatism was rampant and it appeared that our enemy was self-destructing. I did not have to be schooled on this point; a delay by us would be advantageous. I knew these people; there was deep-rooted internecine hatred and mistrust. All the petty squabbles, slights, broken contracts, and perceived thefts would fervently boil into a cauldron of desperation and individual self-preservation. If what I was hearing was true, and it would be very hard to fake all these reports, then the battle was won.

Three different factions had sent word that they were with us and against the leadership in Mecca, one of the factions I found hard to believe. The Jews still under the aging Aaron the Wise's control were easy to believe. The grain merchants guild being on our side was also easy to understand; they were very steady and logical and looked at things long term. The third faction was my old nemesis the Dhinnah family. I did not know how to take this, I had looked forward to wiping these miserable, conniving, camel thieves from the face of the earth. You could never trust what they were saying, even here, but if Mustafa the Angry did rebel in our favor, or even only withhold aid to the Meccan forces, it would make our victory far easier and I wanted as few casualties on our side as possible. They were not totally stupid and the bloody mark was on the sheep; they knew what was in store for them if we achieved victory. War and survival can make odd matfellows, and at this point all help, even from those horrible scorpion-like sneak thieves, was welcomed.

The white flag of truce came with three officers who stated that a cessation of hostilities was still possible if we did not want to fight. This was a convoluted, fancy way of saying surrender and we got word back to them that Mohammad would decide and propose conditions and deliver them in two days. I wanted them to stew and to feel relieved so the harsh terms of surrender would seem more generous. We also stated that we wanted a small delegation from each faction to come to our camp for individual talks at midday on the next day. I knew that this would cause more consternation and infighting, but at the end they would all come. They had to.

Like sheep, group after group came, and they were all to every last man jack of them, our allies. It was ridiculous, but I decided that we would just saunter in on the next day around midday without formal terms of surrender. We informed all the factions together in a group meeting, before they returned to Mecca, that we were to be treated as conquering heroes when we would march into Mecca the next day. It would be a fait accompli and to singularly oppose us in any way would be both futile as well as suicidal.

The next day the army of Allah splendidly and lustrously marched in to the loud joyous cheers and celebrations of the demoralized citizens of the defeated city. There were a couple of old scores I could not let go, but I would not even harm a single member of our new allies, the Dhinnah clan. They, with their evil, cunning ways, could become quite useful as servants to the Servant of Allah, their new commander, the wise Prophet of the one true god Allah. Allah be praised, Allah be praised, Allah be praised.

CHAPTER FORTY-THREE

The New Order

Basically, we just marched in and took over. There were some logistical problems, but we quickly had orders issued and no one objected loudly enough to be heard.

We wanted a certain continuity to memorialize our long standing Mecca connection. We went right back into our old complex, gave the Dhinnah family a couple of hours to clear out, and promised them compensation in a few days. Two weeks later they received back the same fire sale money that they had given us when we had so swiftly fled Mecca. I waited the two weeks to be sure that they did not squawk in any way. There had not been a peep from our new fast friends so I sent the shekels.

To make absolutely sure that everyone completely understood the situation as to who was running things, on the day following our grand triumphant victory, I had three Meccans, on flimsy and obviously trumped up charges, in the main square at high noon, publicly beheaded. These were old scores being settled. The first was a rumor mongering blabbermouth, who would viciously say anything, or slander anyone, to get a little attention. The second was a former servant of ours who had a friend buy his freedom, I later became convinced that the servant had embezzled his freedom money from us. The third case was more personally satisfying, a muscular stout fellow, between 30 and 35, who had a real mean streak in him, and a perverted nature who enjoyed physically hurting women, especially the most vulnerable and most easily abused of women, whores. A coward with men, he had been afraid to rough me up in any way, and was eventually banned from our brothel, but his reputation for inflicting sadistic pain on women, was well known and widely verified. I, and I am sure many other women, enjoyed watching his fat head hit the sand face first with a weak bounce. So the first, a blabbermouth would get to be the momentary center of attention, as the second bought, with his ill-gotten shekels, his total freedom from this world. With the third, I had the executioner instructed to have this sicko piece of camelshit observe the immediate previous decapitations, and then slightly elongate the ceremony, so he was allowed to linger and contemplate the bullying of him, where he had no control over his impending big hurt. Everyone could observe the pusillanimous terror in his eyes, as the truly just sentence was carried out.

There was also a fourth, who was on our unpublished list, Samir the Seasnake, but he was smart enough to have made himself very scare. How the Seasnake managed to live to see his 40th year amazed me and everyone else. This cheat was capable of anything and everything. In a region of double-dealing, lying, back-stabbing scorpions, Samir was the king rat. He lived a charmed life, and had several scars that testified to the many attempts to end his life. If he had been born slightly honest, he would have been far more dangerous, but he was, at least temporarily, saved by his foresight and the divine mercy of Allah.

Mohammad, in his wisdom, understanding, and love, announced through the execution master, that the great and all-powerful, true and one god, had declared an amnesty for all past transgressions, even cowardice in battle. This merciful pronouncement was read directly after the third head had been publicly severed. Allah was widely praised and hailed for his love and ever-shining heart of compassion. In another surprise, who then came immediately into the square of execution, loudly praising Allah for his wisdom and mercy, but Samir. Both the Seasnake and I knew that his escape from Hell could be very short lived; Samir's camel was racing very close to the quicksand. But I had many other figs to dry and would worry about that slimy serpent later.

I was busier than ever, the first concern was to totally secure and regulate Mecca, the second, to fully and completely control all of Arabia.

Armed squads menacingly, and wildly like devils, raced into every hamlet, port, oasis and market town in southern Arabia. Regulations were read and people were put in charge, as our viceroys, in the name of Allah. We controlled or quickly controlled every grain of sand on the peninsula, as well as the western side of the Red Sea, a little bit of the Levant, and a few posts east of the peninsula. With a marginalized Mecca merged into us, no one else in the region stood a chance of independent survival. We seized, co-opted, bulldozed, or cajoled everybody and everything within reach. Any opposition was quickly and unmercifully eradicated. The sands of Arabia might not be much, but they were totally mine, and a base to expand to wherever love of Allah would take us.

I sent for Shahrazad and my sons, who traveled to Mecca slowly in comfort and safety. This time was the happiest of my young life. The old fool was getting more decrepit and easier to control, and my love for Elijah and our sons grew in the warm sunshine of success.

The Jews and Christians were allowed to keep their religions, although they were subtly encouraged to convert, but they all paid the special Jew Tax. The less sophisticated pagans were ordered to convert to Allah, or find a place to go. As a matter of practicality, they had nowhere else to go, so they were forced to convert. Religious courts were established and any convert caught worshipping outside of Islam was executed. I knew that within a generation or two all the very old pagan nonsense would disappear, a mere forgotten whimper within the cacophonous history of religion. Out with the old nonsense and in with the new.

Whereas I had absolute and total control of Islam and the Koran, I was not only the head and moving spirit of the religion, I was actually the living embodiment, I transformed and became the invisible, omnipotent Allah incarnate. I was a living person who many people fervently worshipped in my alter ego as Allah. When I saw the faithful in heartfelt prayer, I felt the power that I possessed. Me, a former child whore, from a family of pimps and whores, had managed to rise to a living deification by my intellect and will. I was the subject of their hopes and desperate aspirations for salvation, and this overwhelming power emboldened and electrified me. The rational me knew that this was ridiculous, but in a sense, I was the only god, I was their salvation, I was Allah.

CHAPTER FORTY-FOUR

Consolidation

These were certainly good years. Elijah and I added two daughters to our clan, and I might add Naomi was banging out babies as well. I just loved stealing all the time I could with my Jewish 'advisor' and confidant. Because of our fairly sudden rise to being a major regional power, things naturally changed.

After a few months of being in Mecca and feeling that the city was totally under the thumb of Allah, Elijah and I, along with our children and Naomi, headed back to Medina. We also took the old drunk and the sissy back with us. I traveled to Mecca every so often to see for my own self that our reports were 100% on target. I wanted to consolidate all of our strength before any further expansion. There were always small wars and rumors of war, but I wanted some internal growth first.

I had an accurate census taken of all men, women, and children as well as a list of the major domesticated animals. We needed more people, camels and horses. Horses were not very good in the desert, but any plans to expand to the more fertile areas would necessitate them.

I set up schools for future horsemen and warriors, and some schools to teach the brightest kids writing and mathematics. In the schools for children under twelve, both boys and girls attended together; after twelve the schools became gender specific. I needed the distaff side of society to become more useful and to gather more respect. This did clash somewhat with our gigantic revenue producing system of brothels, but now well over 90% of women would never be whores. I specifically wanted no intelligent girls to be subjected to the horror that had befallen me, and all brothel inmates were to be treated with a degree of kindness, equity and empathy.

In order to raise revenue, in what I internally called a 'fuck' tax, I banned, through Allah, any futuristic revirginizations. I wanted to control and profit from sex as best I could, the good girls, the vast majority, were to be true virgins until married, and I did what I could to delay the age of marriage. This left the guys with little real access, except at our hugely profit making brothels. I also made female adultery punishable by being stoned to death. I got that idea from the story about Mary Magdalene in the Christian bible, which I had thoroughly studied. If you control sex, alcohol, gambling and food you control men. I needed to control men for our future expansion.

Other powers now sent us diplomats and wanted treaties and mutually beneficial agreements. They also wanted war alliances, but I wanted none of that right now. I needed more Muslims, more camels, and more horses, not less. By running the territory of Arabia correctly with intelligence and honesty, the money was flowing in. I was careful not to squander this much needed capital on palaces or high living, I would rather have a thousand mounted, armored knights than a palace

With all these camels that we did have, I thought that the first expansion would probably be to the Nile valley. I knew that the great river cut through the desert in such a way, because of the annual flood, that it produced the most fertile grain growing area in the world. With its weather and sunshine so very steady, and with a flood that never failed, they always produced a good bountiful harvest. A country that was basically desert supplied half the Mediterranean with grain. If I could control that grain, then I could heavily influence the price of grain. So I knew in which direction we were probably heading.

I made many alliances and friendship treaties through the figurehead, but always insisted on sending Muslims who would tell the people of the wonder and truth of Allah, and his Prophet Mohammad. Everywhere we were getting at least a few converts, secret or open, and my web of information grew.

As a movement we were very lucky. In the world that I knew, no one country dominated. There were mostly smallish states constantly squabbling with one another, and they all wanted to be our friends. It was the perfect timing for a new Rome to develop by conquest. I knew that it was prudent not to move too fast, the figs were there

to be picked, but it was best to wait until they were ripe for
the picking.

CHAPTER FORTY-FIVE

The Revelation

I believed that I was beyond being shocked at the ways of this world. But I found out something that brought together all the loose ends of my existence and showed me the true light. Actually, when I found out, I could not believe that I had not discovered it myself years ago. All of a sudden, that which had been deeply obscured: became insightfully clear, making obvious sense.

It came about this way. I had a very minor physical abnormality, not a big deal physically, functionally, or cosmetically in any way. Because of the life style of myself and other Arabian women, no one but a foot fetish freak would ever know or even suspect. On my left foot, between my second and middle toes was a little extra slim flesh, it was as if I had webbing, like a Red Sea duck, almost half way up between the toes. This was only at the bottom of the foot, that part which would touch the sand, a thin membrane of skin connecting the second and third toes and only on the left side, and only half way up the toes. I hardly ever gave it any thought.

I cannot remember if I even checked the feet of our

little sons Husan and Hussein, but in any event, their toes looked liked everybody else's. It was only when my first daughter Zeynab was born that it reappeared. I had not even looked at her toes; she certainly was a beautiful baby girl. It was Elijah who brought it to my attention. He loved to play with, sometimes slightly roughly like a man's man would do, all of his children and he noticed the small bit of extra flesh. Normally he would not have even mentioned it because of its unimportance, but he had noticed the same thing on his eldest son by Naomi.

Parents do give traits to their children so he figured he had somehow given his children, from both sides of the tent, the same trait. But he knew that his feet were normal. He pondered the fact, checked all his kids and saw the same thing in his just born youngest daughter by Naomi. By now he had eight kids and three had the trait and five did not. I generally shared all my thoughts with Elijah, but I decided that this one time I would make an exception. There was no question that he was the only possible candidate for being my children's father, but politically and within the movement, any talk or suspicion of our love affair could have disastrous results.

I just told him that odd things happen with offspring in both people and animals, and it was no big deal. Inwardly I was not being truthful, as my mind raced and wondered. Ancient questions that I had were resurfacing.

The whole family and top diplomatic people were scheduled to be making an official state visitation to our territory in Yemen, with some stops along the way, so I busied myself with the plans and decisions that had to be made.

Our first major stop was in Mecca where we encamped in the old complex. I should have had horrible memories about the place and have had it razed, but I always looked upon it as the crucible of my practical education and developer of my will. In a weird sense, I thanked the perverted old drunk for the hell he put me through in that complex, because that is what enabled me to rise to a position arguably greater than any other woman who had ever lived. Without the degrading, filthy, sick, atrocities I endured, I would not be ruling Arabia or Islam. I liked having the power, I liked controlling the populace, and I like being able to put my foresight and whims into reality.

After a couple of days I made arrangements and visited my old friend, and my babies' granduncle, Aaron the Wise, still the leader of the Meccan Jewish community. He was getting along in his years but still retained a slight twinkle in his eye. He was also still very sharp intellectually. I saw to it that we were alone, without servants, and after about ten minutes of pleasant remembrances about my early childhood and mathematical games he had taught me, I asked him to be very frank with me as to his understanding of Islam and especially me. I assured him that nothing would be shared with anyone else, no one would be upset, and that his people would in no way suffer for any frankness, but that I must have his true learned opinion on the subjects.

He said to me that he knew that he could trust me and believe me, but that he was sure that I would understand any reticence he might have. I again reassured him of my absolute fidelity and honesty and friendship, but I must know his truthful reflections

He stated, a little bit haltingly, that he thought, no, he almost knew for certain, that I was running the show. He thought that this was remarkable that a woman could do this. He knew of women in history who had come to great prominence, but to do so in Arabia was really hard to believe. In order to again reassure my old friend, and to get him to open up even more, I did relay to him that he was totally correct.

Aaron told me that he was pretty sure that I was writing the Koran, by having Mohammad's words interpreted as I desired. He had been in Mohammad's presence twice during trances and was positive that the verbiage coming forth was not capable of meaningful translation. I informed him that this was also true and that now, where I controlled the ancient lush, I issued statements from Allah that were issued even if Mohammad had not been in a trance; after all who would know. I even informed him that the trances were now less and less frequent and of a shorter time period, all of which was completely accurate.

Aaron then said, "Well, that has been my opinion for a long time, but I have never, and will never, tell anybody else what I have observed in life." I thanked him, but informed him that I wanted to know it all, everything.

He then said to me, "I think that I understand what you are asking; after all, it is like you have a Jewish head. If you are asking what I think you are getting to, the answer is yes, I think so."

I could understand his reluctance to be bluntly forthright. I asked him directly, "Aaron, who do you think my father is?" To which he replied, "I believe, and have always believed, that I am your true father and that you are my daughter!" I got up and devotionally kissed him on both of his cheeks.

He related the story. My late mother had not always been the slovenly, drunken, addicted floozy I had known in childhood and growing up. Aaron bespoke of a fair, sweet, lovely girl prostituted by a mean drunken husband who showed her little to no respect. When my mother was a regular brothel inmate, before her legal marriage and revirginization, Aaron developed, and it was a mutual development, love for this unfortunate girl. After my three surviving sisters were born, times were difficult because of gambling debts, which threatened the entire family, Mohammad, who well knew of the attraction, leased my mother to Aaron for three months. She went to his household ostensibly as a bookkeeper/translator for a few hours everyday. I was born about eleven months after this arrangement started. Aaron explained that it was far better for my mother to be his exclusive concubine for the contracted period, because a far worse fate was in store for her if Mohammad could not raise the money this way.

Aaron sadly declared that, after the arrangement's three months time was over, he wanted to extend or to even possibly buy my mother, but Mohammad was doing better so all deals were off. My mother, Aaron continued, went rapidly downhill physically, and emotionally after that. "The woman you knew growing up was not the same woman a few years earlier. Her spirit had been broken and she retreated to alcoholism and narcotic substances." he longingly recalled.

I asked him about the skin flap and he took off his left sandal and showed me his. "I always knew you were my daughter and that is why I would never engage you at the brothel; it is an abomination, and an unforgivable sin against god, for a father to have sex with his daughter!" At this point I broke completely down and cried like I have never cried before, never in childhood or never in the pain of childbirth. It was as if my tears washed away some of the horrors of my life, that my soul was cleansed of its agony and filth by waves of compassion, truth and true humanity.

I walked with gusto into the sunshine of kindness and love for the first time, I felt a rebirth, as if every cloud and horrible confining emotion had been liberated from my internal essence, the pith of my humanity, from my soul. Finally, it all made sense. Before that day, which I shall always treasure as my revelation day, I could not have hated Mohammad more. Now, if anything, I hated him less. If anything, I hated everybody and everything less. My life, for the first time, made some sense. For the first time, I felt whole, completed, and unrestrained.

How could I, with my intelligence, be that moron's child! Oh happy day – I was not part of him, I should have seen it before now, but thank Allah, Buddha & Christ that I not only saw, but received total verification from my true father, the aptly named Aaron the Wise, while he still lived. Everything fell into place, I was dropped into Mohammad's household, but thankfully I was not of his blood. It were as if scales had obscured my eyes, but now they were miraculously lifted and I could again see. I cannot get across how wonderful I felt! I had never known, never knew I could even feel, such an all-powerful, expansionist, wonderful, fulfilling presence of love. Verily, as of that moment, a new Fatima, and a better Fatima, emerged from the ashes of degradation and filth, and I was spiritually reborn into a glistening new world.

CHAPTER FORTY-SIX

The Road to Yemen

It was hard for me to keep up with the old routines. Even though I had this massive change I did not want to tip my hand in any way. I wanted and needed some time to reflect upon my new understanding and reformulate my actions. This long journey to Yemen and back was a good period to ponder on the meaning of life, exactly what was important, and what my role as Allah's embodiment should be.

There was no question that we were getting stronger. By running the regional empire with intelligence and honesty our power grew. Corruption and especially, petty everyday corruption, is the enemy of good government, and I had made it a top priority to break the old systems, to run the state as corruption free as possible. With the twin forces of Islam and the executioner's long sword, examples were made to show that corrupt favors, double dealing, and governmental theft were folly. No matter who you were, or what your family connections were, if you stole from the people or Allah, it was your last act upon this earth before an ignoble death.

Trade flourished, new enterprises were encouraged and started, even marginal land was being put into crops or pasture. It was very odd and a gigantic irony, but Islam was very good for the people. Belief in a being, who never existed, actually brought prosperity, fairness and a greater feeling of security. Outside of the occasional skirmish here and there, our young men were not being killed or maimed in battle. Life was not good just for me, and my relations, but it was good for almost everyone in Arabia. It was not totally universal, but for the first time a very high percentage of people were leading satisfied lives.

On the long journey to Yemen, done mostly along the Red Sea coast, I formulated my plans as the pleasant seascapes slowly rolled by. I, who had been brutalized and terrorized, pledged that I would become the savior of the brutalized, the terrorized, and all of mankind. A degraded child prostitute, from a truly sick, disgusting family, would uplift humanity and spread the wings of joy and love. I would do this for all of society, especially raising the least among us. I could understand the omnipresent powerlessness of the outcasts, the slaves, the whores, the damaged, the no-hopers. Everyone, with the possible exception of the richest and most mighty; would live a better life. This was the vision that vigorously unfolded to me on that long voyage to Yemen.

My mind raced with many ideas on how to accomplish everything that I wished to implement for the universal betterment of our species. I was in love with life and felt an inner joy that I had never before come close to experiencing. Even the air that I breathed, as it billowed into my nostrils and cascaded into and then out of my lungs, felt sweetly life empowering and engendered, a much appreciated, inner peace.

CHAPTER FORTY-SEVEN

My Dream

By the end of the long journey, as we arrived back in Medina, my plans were highly organized. Plans are always subject to change and refinement, but the building stones were in place.

My main concern was how to perpetuate my vision after my death. Although I was still relatively young, I foresaw a thousand year realm. If humankind could not progress after 1000 years of fairness and prosperity, then the entire scheme was hopeless from its beginning. Mohammad was not long for this world, and that was apparent to anybody who had direct contact with him. His dissolute life had robbed him of his health and what little intelligence he had been born with. I could survive the figurehead's death. It had already been published and sanctified that the big swish, my husband Ali, was the Prophet's spiritual heir, as well as his cousin, adopted son and son-in-law. Ali could be easily controlled by flattery, along with cute pre-adolescent boys. If he did step out of line, a simple threat would work wonders; I anticipated no problems with the big baby. Upon Ali's demise, whether timely or not, my sons would be first in line, and if young, they would even need a regent.

It would be far harder to control after my death, but I should have at least a few decades to set Islam up so it could thrive in peace and prosperity. If that really could be accomplished, then other lands would be easily co-opted into the fold. He who has the gold makes the rules, and the country that has the prosperity has many friends and allies.

Through Mohammad's numerous trances, the Koran added many new verses. Charity was given the highest priority and rules about fairness and true equity were promulgated. I had medicine encouraged and a big new school of medicine established. It was true that current medicine had little efficacy, but people wanted to be treated and hoped that it helped. It was my desire that the medical schools might actually improve health to the point where medicine would in fact make people better. The way medicine worked when I was young was analogous to praying to Allah, neither really did any good, but people felt better if they believed in it. With medicine though, it might actually magnify itself to a point where people were actually helped.

New verses in the Koran allowed slavery, but discouraged it being imposed on true believers. It became a blessing to free slaves by will or while still alive; and no slaves could be forcibly raped, maimed, or killed, except under certain specific conditions. I also put in a verse that no slave could testify in a court of law unless he were free and not subject to an owner's wrath.

The biggest thing I did for slaves was the Koranic verses where any slave had the right to purchase his or her freedom at a fair price. A local official would set a fair price if there was a dispute; a slave could borrow money and be legally bound to pay it back to purchase his freedom. This was true for all slaves; men, women, and children, as long as the slaves were Muslims.

I considered long and hard on how to integrate women fairly into society. It became law that married women and single women whose fathers were alive could own property in their own names. Children could not be taken from a mother without court approval, which had been a common practice and threat from unhappy husbands. Mohammad's verses proclaimed that husbands could not murder their wives or sell them into slavery or prostitution; and that women could testify in court and hold all jobs and positions. These steps were just a beginning, but were intended to curb some of the brutal behavior women had lived under. There were passages on treating all Muslims, including children, with kindness and respect.

I wanted a feeling of Islamic community and brotherhood to overtake the tribal ethos that prevailed in Arabia and caused such bloodshed and tragedy. If everyone could look upon a fellow follower as a close relative, then society would be the victor. I wanted the religion to sponsor kindness, a kindness tempered by mercy. It became a blessing not only to help your relatives but also the poor, the sick, the elderly and all those who, for whatever reason, needed assistance.

I was not high on narcotics; I well knew the difficulties my plans presented. But any nudge toward civility was a step toward the oasis. The goals of fellowship had to be somewhat vague, but they were put in the Koran as a backdrop to the idealized Islamic State, perhaps unobtainable, but something that society could strive toward.

So by setting a tone of mutual cooperation and respect, and by prohibiting the absolute worst current practices, I was hoping to romance the populace to a better place for everyone.

These ideas and laws came from me, but were not intended to help me in any way. I could not go back and show kindness to a child named Fatima who was about to be brutalized and viciously traumatized. But, hopefully I could help children, living and as yet unborn, from the terror and egregiously psychotic assaults that I had faced. The irony was that it took my hurts, fears, and total pathetic degradation, for me to empathize with these future victims and, with luck, be able to rectify the horror that they now would not be subject to. In an odd way, Mohammad's legacy could be a kind world based upon his unfeeling, drunken and sick brutality. Ironically, out of his cauldron of filth and atrocity, perhaps a better world could emerge.

CHAPTER FORTY-EIGHT

Deaths

Many have observed that life appears to go in cycles, while the specter of death comes in bunches. I know that it sounds self-serving, grandiose and egotistical, but I was truly working very hard with the goal of the betterment of all humanity. I am proud to say this was bearing fruit, and there was a new general happiness and prosperity throughout all the lands I controlled. Babies were being born in record numbers, and the average shepherd, merchant, and camelman seemed to be more prosperous and lived a more happy fulfilling life. Even death was carrying off fewer souls.

Because of circumstances beyond Arabia, the treasury of Allah received a substantial influx of much needed gold. There were two wars going on in the northern Sahara region. The first concerned a long-standing and bitter dispute for control of the far western region, where carnage, cruelty, and desperation were victorious in a horrible long series of battles and raids. The second was closer to home. The fertile Nile valley, a perennial source of abundant golden grain, was in a war of attrition with forces to its immediate west. These wars and consequential slaughter of men, horses, and camels caused temporary shortages of war material and huge price swings.

The king of Egypt, still sometimes referred to as the Pharaoh, decided it was imperative to obtain more adult camels to send off to the slaughter of war. He had gold and grain and we managed to round up 4,000 of the beasts. They were mostly middle-aged animals, and we received a price that a year before would almost have purchased 10,000 very healthy camels. They received the camels and we received enough grain to be forced to build new granaries and a fortune in gold. We were, for the present, short of camels, but I kept almost all of the young adult females. We could purchase more, if necessary, from the northeast toward the Fertile Crescent at lower prices if we could not wait until the natural increase came about. The treasury made most of the money, but shekels were spread around to almost every camel owner and merchant on the peninsula.

We also were able to use the wars for another doubly good purpose. I had intentionally kept our army small to save the expense and to have more civilian males in regular productive jobs. However, we had an opportunity here that was too good to pass up. We formed a large volunteer division of infantry and archers of young men 16 to 21 years old. I wanted boys who had not seen combat, who would become battle hardened and were young enough to be around for a long active time in the reserves, in case we were ever attacked. We supplied our own sergeants and officers as well as all the equipment. This was a tailor made division rented out on a monthly basis to the king of Egypt for a very large sum of money. We also received death compensation for each and every death no matter how it occurred. The death compensation went to the soldier's family and we had, through female scribes, accurate information on each and every member of the division. If 120 soldiers died during a month we sent in 120 replacements. I deliberately had woman scribes and record keepers so that these young men could see women doing responsible, intelligent work. The treasury did very well.

So, we were becoming very rich and the regional powerhouse. Even if Egypt won its war, it would become at least partially Finlandized; Islam was growing in wealth and power, and we were far less likely to be attacked. But the history of the world seems to say that these blissful moments of prosperity and contentment can never last too long. I went through my worse personal tragedy and period of deep depression.

Normally a birth of a child, a son, is the time of greatest celebration. After two successive daughters, I was eager to add one more son to our family, which I shared with my true husband Elijah. All my previous pregnancies had gone without a single jackal lurking about, and this one did too. But after the long wait, and welcoming difficult throes of childbirth, my son, our son, my little man - was born still. He looked perfect, healthy, and beautiful, but there was no life in him. Before this, I could not understand the grief that other women had spoken of upon the birth of a dead child. Now I fully knew that tragedy of motherhood.

I entered deepest despair. It was the new Fatima, the one who had received enlightenment, who could now experience horrible anguish. I know that before my revelation day, I was not capable of entering the void and nihilistic yearning that overtook my soul. My growth had paradoxically caused my utter misery and hopelessness. Could only a mother feel the sad nothingness that I felt? I did not know. Intellectually I knew it should not have been such a staggering loss, but as a mother I knew what I felt. I observed that some of the men snickered at my profound reaction to my grief, I did not care, I did not care about much of anything. I only knew what I felt. As the ironies in this world piled up on me, my greatest happiness transformed me to a point where I could feel far worse than I did when a hardened girl had the horrors of this world fall upon her. I suffered far more than my brief son, who was but a momentary flicker upon the sands of time.

Shortly after the death of my third son, I received news from Mecca that my real father, Aaron the Wise, had peacefully lapsed into death. I was sad, but he had lived a long, productive life, and I had learned what I had to learn from him before he passed on. I was so very proud that my true, all be it secret, father had managed to live his long life with great respect, intelligence, and above all else, the pervasive dignity that he always enjoyed. Because of viewing men like my true father and contrasting the horrific existence of my putative father Mohammad, burdened with filth, greed, craziness, perversion, ugliness, cruelty, stupor, and stupidity; my one highest quest in life was to live with, be surrounded by, and have my life imbued with dignity. Anyone observing my situation could easily understand my need, desire, and yearning for that one elusive quality; to lead the good life, to lead the dignified life, to live within a circle of dignity.

Aaron was certainly older than Mohammad, but until the last bit of life he had seemed younger. I hoped that besides his intelligence, I had inherited Aaron's long and healthy physiology. I would have bet on the old drunken sodomite going first, but that was not to be.

The next death was surprising, and a blessing that it followed Aaron's rather than preceding it. Naomi, my fellow wife, sister, and friend died in childbirth. Fortunately her daughter survived and Elijah gave the girl a Latin name that bespoke of the tears and anguish at the girl's birth – Dolores. There was much sadness in my household, but I knew I had to carry on. The movement, now energized with the new goal of altruism, was far more important than any one person or family. Everything had to be sacrificed to bring the people to enlightenment, to enter into the realm of the good life.

All deaths create disruptions, but the next one was truly world changing. The death of Jesus, magnificent in its agony and gore eventually transformed the world via Christianity. The death of the Prophet, at this moment in time, profoundly reversed the course of Islam, and hence the course of history.

CHAPTER FORTY-NINE

The Death of the Messenger of Allah

The precarious health of the Prophet had been noticed and quietly commented on by everyone who had seen him. As Mohammad sank deeper into decrepitude, he was well hidden from public view.

His body shrank and his hair thinned as a permanent forward bend in his spine advanced with age. Even his voice, always a little squeaky, rose in pitch, he walked with his legs more separated to compensate for a greater imbalance. He claimed he was constantly full of aches and pains, as he drank intoxicants continuously toward the goal of oblivion. The end could not be too distant.

His lifelong immodesty concerning sexual acts refused to abate, even when it caused widespread household derision because of his total impotence. He still went through the motions of trying to bugger eight-year-old boys, but with his sexual member dangling lifelessly limp for the household world to see and be amused.

He lost all control over his belching and puking and would loudly wheeze in an effort to coax breathe into his lungs. The Prophet lost all pride about urinating anywhere as his control appeared to diminish to the state of non-existence. Never again would he enjoy an arched flow, but only a leaky spout without force.

All these bodily problems paled when compared to the problem of Mohammad's shit. Now, at any time, at any place, in front of anyone liquid streams of yellow-brown pungent shit would ooze down his legs, as he apparently would carry on with whatever, as if there was no concern. He was the only one who could not smell his own stink.

Adult sized diapers were tried, but he often refused to keep them on. Four servants were employed with the exclusive assignment of cleaning up Mohammad, his clothing, and everything that he befouled. Unfortunately the nickname 'Baby Shithouse' had received wide circulation within the compound. Perversely, when he would wear his diapers, and wanted to be changed, he would hold up one finger for piss or two fingers for the other, and hold a wide grin as his keepers went into action. At other times he would just drop the diapers and hold up two fingers while he wiggled his butt indicating that he wanted to be wiped, which had to be done in quickstep, or he would drag his ass across the rug or anything else that was handy.

Needless to say the Messenger of Allah caused smells and gaseous explosions that never could be gotten used to. The entire household was happiest when he was asleep, drunk with his bottle beside him, merely making smelly farts every now and then.

As a policy decision, I only allowed his clothing to be washed so many times. I was very afraid of someone, outside of the knowledge, seeing him wearing linen with an obvious yellow-brown stain on the backside. So after a few wearings and the degrading of the cloth, I had his clothing burned, thereby removing any evidence of the lifestyle of the Prophet. Even the incineration of the cloth produced more foul odors. Thank Allah for the desert winds that generally carried the noxious smells off, but I had to keep four groups of unkempt camels surrounding the complex to help explain any passing stench.

There were days when he must have been cleaned up twenty times, only to piss himself five minutes later. It was a constant struggle and losing battle, but he had to be maintained. The longer the old pervert stayed from the gates of Hell, the longer the Koran could be easily altered. The largest battle was keeping any talk of his true condition from becoming general knowledge.

His habits varied, but generally he drank during the night and slept through a large portion of the day. One particular day he was asleep at the general household's awakening and still asleep as sunset was rolling around. A maid, with the normal dinner portion, attempted to awaken him and could only gauge that he was alive. I was sent for and observed that he was beyond a normal drunken state. Eventually he gained some consciousness, and his famous appetite came through, as he allowed the servants to spoon-feed him some lamb stew. He complained loudly of all types of physical problems, and was exasperated by my order that he was to drink no alcohol until he recovered. He was constantly cleaned as every orifice discharged some type of disgusting stuff. He lapsed in and out of total consciousness and into full delirium. He began talking, or a better word might be ranting, about flying elephants and camels, which were accurately dumping huge amounts of fecal material upon the heads of his many enemies. The Messenger of Allah laughed and laughed while telling and retelling this tale, as he made noises simulating the sounds of these huge shit bombs landing on the selected heads of his unfortunate enemies. His speech then became harder to hear, and very difficult to comprehend, because of its slurring and ever changing pitch. It was not the usual gibberish, but something where words could be individually understood, but made even less sense than his normal drunken tirades.

As far as I was concerned this repetitive nonsense was more source material for the Koran. Since the utterances were devoid of reason, no one else could make out any sense of the ramblings. I would interpret them later. He actually was in this agitated waking sleep for sometime as his body befouled everything in all directions. He finally stopped the jabbering and very shortly after that he stopped his heavy breathing. All around him people were looking at him and each other. After one-half to three-quarters of a minute a loud gulp of air was drawn in that startled the tense onlookers, and he eerily started a heavily belabored rhythm of breath.

This cycle of a stopping and restarting of breathing repeated itself once more, as the small entourage could feel life slipping away from Islam's most important citizen. Each breath sounded as if it were a struggle. Then an extremely loud, very long, gaggingly putrid fart filled the air with poisonous gas. It was as if his body ripped itself in half, and all the decaying, festering smells inside his rotting internal cavity were liberated to befoul the world. This man, old camelbreath, who had lived his life in filth and stink, ended his life with the biggest and ugliest fart ever known to strike Arabia. People fled in all directions, you could not breathe it in. How appropriate it was that Mr. Stink died in a hellhole of vomit inducing, unbreathable, obnoxious, gaseous stench. Every person within the room could never forget the death rattling end of the Prophet of Allah, and the ugly noxious gases thrust forth from his now useless body. The room had to be closed and redone to the point where it would have been easier to burn the room down and start over again.

The reality of death soon set in; there would finely be no more folly from this fool.

CHAPTER FIFTY

Burial Games

I had prepared for the Messenger of Allah's death in many ways, but certain things could not have been foreseen or planned. The burial would be no problem and would follow the usual course, only on a gigantic scale. I had a burial gown made several years previously, and I had it altered just one month before the death to reflect the shrunken state of the wearer. He would be buried in a perfectly clean, brand new costume befitting the Servant of Allah.

The problem was the power struggle that erupted as soon as word of the Prophet's demise hit the streets. I did not realize how many people and factions were eagerly awaiting the big moment. All of a sudden it was do or die for control of the movement, with all the accompanied wealth and power.

Even though it was planned to enthrone my nominal husband, Ali, as the leader, other ambitious souls were jumping for joy at the chance of grabbing the gold and the power. The problem was that Ali, with age, was exhibiting even less gravitas. Everybody who had any personal contact with him was left with the impression that he was a dandi-fied crybaby, with less will than the average pre-pubescent boys that he was so famous for lusting after. Normal ten year olds had more balls and the average housewife had more hair on her chest; he was such a wimpy, effeminate weakling.

Several candidates were obviously jockeying for the fastest jackal, and the strongest was none other than Aisha's father, Abe Bakr. Naturally the grieving widow of Mohammad had no time to grieve, she only had time to intrigue on behalf of her father. Abe immediately came out with the sacred conversation he and his son-in-law Mohammad had, witnessed by Aisha, that Ali was still too young to immediately become the Iman. Abe reported that Mohammad had commanded that the Iman must always be over 50 years old, and that Abe was currently the best candidate over 50. This was pure and unadulterated camelcrap, but because of Ali's obvious impediments, it gave their side a camel to ride.

Abe proposed that a grand council should immedi-ately meet after the funeral and elect an Iman to guide Islam. I rallied my supporters in an effort to forestall that action, and have the position go to the intended heir, Ali. There was a lot of activity and tension as people shucked and jived before the funeral, but it was still only talk and maneuvering without any bloodshed.

The grand, magnificent funeral was held for the per-verted drunk, like he had been Allah's Messenger to a grateful world. Person after person waxed long and loudly on the wonderful life of the greatest man ever to bless Arabia. I had to control my puke response as I listened to this offal, while holding a hopeful smile. It was only after the funeral that the heavy games began and the long knives unsheathed.

Abe, all on his own without consulting anybody, organized a caucus of men to vote on a new Iman. Naturally he invited all the leading figures, as well as many minor league officials whose votes he thought he controlled. Ali received an invitation. The meeting was scheduled in three days time after the funeral, to be held at a large eating/drinking complex owned by one of Abe's nephews. There was no question that Abe would be crowned at this packed caucus.

I issued orders, through Ali, that attendance at any such meeting was illegal and a deadly insult to Islam. Then I issued Mohammad's last additions to the Koran, which spoke of Mohammad's upcoming death and the passing of the torch of Islam to his heir Ali.

Two hours before the scheduled meeting, I had troops loyal to my regime, placed inside the meeting place to prevent any gathering. That night at midnight, Abe had a much smaller group meet at an oasis four miles from Medina, and surprise, surprise, he was unanimously elected by this rump parliament of his stooges.

Abe encamped on the north side of the city, attracted various army units and a semi-armed moblike rabble of irregulars. I, with Ali, was in the middle and southern part of Medina with my loyal troops and support. It looked like imminent blood would be shed between rival Muslims as the beginning of the deadly Sunni and Shiite split was born. Many troops, on both sides, fled from their units to join the opposing army. It was easy for everybody to gain information, and it appeared that both sides were roughly equal in strength.

There were surprises though. My slick trick Obama had left Africa and had just come into Medina with a slave train of Nubian brothel fodder; he and his brother Osama were captains in Abe's constabulary. I felt so betrayed by my former screw buddies and business partners. They were biting the hands of those who had raised and protected them. At this point people from all over the peninsula were arriving in Medina to join one side or the other. It was truly a real big, ugly mess.

During these goings on I received a message from Shahrazad that Samir the Seasnake desperately wanted to see me. I informed her that I was busy, and to tell him to leave a message, but Shahrazad said that the Seasnake insisted on seeing me personally, it was a matter or life or death, and that time was of the essence.

I knew that Abe, as with almost everybody else who was prominent in Arabia, detested the Seasnake. I suffered him to be presented.

I opened with, "I know you said it was a matter of life

or death, and on that point you are correct. What is so important."

He immediately, after a few obligatory compliments and professions of admiration and loyalty, cut the camelcrap and went into his spiel. "I want nothing but your friendship and possible consideration at a later time. I must tell you of a plot on your life." He was very specific on an attempt that was going to be immediately made to poison me and named two lower level kitchen staff, who were in league with the poisoner. Samir knew for a fact that this assassination was the brainchild of Abe Bakr. I thanked him, but said that for sometime I had taken precautions and that I had my own food taster.

He said that was widely known, and they had worked their way around that roadblock; I was certainly in a mood to listen to what he had to say. He related that the food taster, a woman my age and size, was not part of the plot. Abe had gotten hold of a new poison from India that was very deadly, but its victims showed no signs of bodily distress for at least one hour, sometimes two hours, before they quickly sickened and died a horrible death.

In a coincidence of perfect timing, as Samir was finishing his talk, a servant came in and announced that dinner was ready. My dinner and food taster came in a few minutes later as the food was laid out for the taster to eat. Samir was still with me as I told the taster to eat heartily. When I had watched her eat some of all the dishes, I told her to go into the ante-room and wait as I resumed with the Seasnake.

He said that he did not know exactly when the attack on me would be, but that it would definitely come within a few days. I informed him that I wanted him to stay at a certain place within the complex; he bowed and said that he would await further instructions. He was capable of anything including trying to poison me himself, and then becoming my Munchausen by proxy savior to reap a large reward. This was unlikely because he did fear death and he knew that I was no fool. I figured he was probably sincere, and the evidence was good enough to refrain from eating for a few hours. I generally had been too lazy and incautious with my food, and usually partook right after the taster finished. I wanted to wait and see what happened. If there were traitors in my staff, I wanted to be totally sure and then have them exposed and publicly tortured to death.

Like clockwork, about one hour after the meal was served, a servant came rushing in with the news that the taster was ill and looked terrible. I went to her to ascertain if she had eaten anything else, and, in her agony, she assured me that she had not. She must have felt death rushing in upon her, because she asked me to promise to take care of her one son; at that point she began to shake violently and was quickly dead. I had missed death by about fifteen minutes. I found it another irony that my life was saved by the most untrustworthy man in the kingdom.

The Medina Standoff

Ali was nominally in charge of our army and that was not good. By the nature of developments, he had to be somewhat out there, but he did not make a virile commander as he was obviously scared to death and so wimpy and girlish. I could easily predict the slaughter of our household, and the end of all that I had worked for, as well as the future betterment of mankind, amid the yelping sounds of crazed young soldiers, wildly slashing with bloody scimitars. We might win, but the problem was it appeared more of our troops were deserting to Abe than the trickle we were now getting from the north side.

I did not want a blood bath for obvious reasons, and it appeared that Abe did not either for the reason of legitimization. If he slaughtered the Prophet's family in a bloody frenzy, he would lose many of his followers, and be hated by many devoted adherents to the point of having to fear assassination attempts. That did not hinder his huge desire to become Iman, with all the perks and power he desperately craved.

He sent Obama over as an envoy under a flag of truce,

and I met with my former friend. I did not think it was the wisest choice for an agent, but this was business. Abe wanted me to be the recipient of the discussion, so it made me think that the little dummy Aisha had finally seen enough to realize that I was controlling the situation.

Ali and I, together met with Obama, and after the usual claptrap, he said that compromise was still possible and desirable. In short, Abe wanted to be the Iman, but would publicly state that Ali was to take over after the spot became open, as long as Ali had reached 50 years of age. Ali was 33 at the time, so it would be a long time in coming, and we all know how very cheap life can be in Arabia. Ali, I, and all factions, would solemnly swear fealty to Abe, and we would sit and wait for the long time to slowly pass. As part of the deal, we would continue to keep everything that we possessed, as well as enjoy all the honors and social positions that we held.

I do not think that Abe, and certainly not the bubble brained Aisha, realized how much gold was in my possession. I had come to the conclusion that we would probably lose a fight, and this deal sounded okay, when you considered the alternative. I told Obama to go back, but to return again tomorrow with Abe, under a personal guarantee of safety from both Ali and me, and we could hopefully conclude all the recent unpleasantries.

On the next day, the only thing that we demanded to be included into the deal was that Ali would immediately become the sub-Iman, a little bit like being the crown prince, since it was Ali, perhaps more like being the clown prince, or then again, perhaps more like a clown princess. In any event, the agreement was reached, and a joint statement was made, which included a full amnesty for all actions by anybody prior to the announcement of the mutual agreement. I already had completed the task of having the offending kitchen staff heavily flogged and then beheaded at sunrise on the same day, in the front outside area of the complex, with all the servants and staff in attendance. One of the honored guests had apparently died during the flogging, but we went through with the beheading anyway.

In actuality the arrangement, more or less, worked as promised, and I settled in as the doubly glorified wife of the Iman elect and daughter of the late Prophet.

On the night that the food taster died in her service to Allah, I allowed Samir the Seasnake his freedom from his confinement, plus a reasonably generous reward for his very timely information. About six weeks after that incident, when the truce was working well, or so it seemed, Shahrazad again came to me with a request for another audience made by the Seasnake.

I immediately granted this request. I was interested; his previous visit completely changed the course of, my now much longer, life. But if this were merely a request for extra money, he would be severely disappointed. He came forth, and with less preliminary formalities, informed me that the new Iman had put into place a new plan to kill me off:

actually a new plan for me to unfortunately die a natural death. I was a tad surprised, but certainly not shocked. I knew the personalities and the totality of circumstances, Arabia is after all the world leader in duplicitous intrigue.

This second plan involved my loyal friend and long time, if seldom used, personal physician Muammar. The Seasnake told me that the doctor was very reluctant to agree, but was forced to go along, because a refusal would have resulted in Muammar's and his entire family's immediate death. Muammar was ordered that as soon as I became ill or injured, or if I became pregnant, that he would make sure that I was given pills, which would accidentally kill me or I would die in childbirth, which was still quite common. With Abe dead set on assassinating me, even if I somehow skirted around this second attempt, sooner or later, he would get lucky and find a way. I had no doubt that Samir was being sincere, because unfortunately it all did make sense.

I knew that I had to stay healthy and formulated a long term plan. I was not ready to be buried, with great pomp and ceremony, next to dear old dad.

CHAPTER FIFTY-TWO

Mucking the Cards

I was both literally and figuratively sick, and I certainly could not call for my physician. Basically I had had it with all the intrigue and camelcrap that I had put up with for years. My life was a total deception and lie and I was so tired of all the duplicitous prevarications that my old life demanded from me. The power to help the world had been, at least temporarily, stolen from me, and I had another very creditable assassination threat looming next door. I had cared about the movement, and then my heartfelt attempt to uplift humanity to the zenith of having life really worth living for most people. My reforms that had already been put into place were being countermanded one after another by the new Iman. All the old male chauvinistic camelshit was being rapidly reinstated by this aging pig of a man, Abe Bakr, who was just one step above, and in the same mold, as the late Messenger of Pigshit. I was very disheartened and weary, and I was sick to death of having to publicly smile at, and be in the vicinity of, my sickening, sicko fag husband.

I had to do something; I just could not wait around

until Muammar or some other assassin would join the conspiracy and terminate my still young life. I wrestled with a lot of options, plans and thoughts, and none seemed to be adequate until I turned a mental corner and decided that the only way was for me to get real selfish. I had to make some large sacrifices, but I had to put the here and now of Fatima first. For the first time in my life I had to screw the ambition, goals and the movement, and concentrate solely on me, and my safety. The thought of being murdered in an evil conspiracy and then being solemnly buried next to that slovenly, sickening, sodomite, so aptly named Baby Shithouse, just made me want to puke buckets.

Abe was no kid and not particularly healthy so there was a good chance that he might turn belly up at any moment, but that would not help me tremendously. Ali was still far from 50 and other wannabe Imans would be popping up like sand fleas and shoving themselves to the front of the line. I would probably be perceived as a threat to any new leader, and I had to get out of sight and out of mind, and I meant way out of sight and way out of mind.

The toughest part was our children. They were probably safe in Medina with me out of the picture, and would continue to be raised as young honored royals. Sadly, we would have to leave them, but all of us, including my children, would be safer and better off. In my life, I have had to make some tough decisions, and this was by far the toughest, but there was no question that in the long run it was the best decision, the only real way. The children were all very bright and receiving fine educations. They almost assuredly, being the Prophet's grandchildren, would rise to great prominence in Medina. I was so proud and happy that I had bright kids, no part of the dull witted family of Mohammad and Ali. The continued ironies of life, the kids had already thriven under the aegis of being Mohammad's grandchildren, while avoiding the curse of the inferior blood of Mohammad. They had the best of both worlds, the supposed relationship to a famous man, and the actual total distance from any true connection with the drunken, perverted moron.

So I speedily put my plan together. Elijah and I, as well as all his children through my true sister Naomi; set off for a trip to the East, ostensibly to Muscat near the peninsula's southeastern corner. We were accompanied by Shahrazad, some loyal servants, a troop of 20 bodyguards, and more than enough gold to last five lifetimes. The trip was officially just a visit, but we had to flee as quickly as possible. Elijah informed people that he was moving to Muscat permanently and would hitch a ride with me, although nobody much cared what he was doing. Muscat itself was an ugly, hot, dry backward town in an intellectual sea of ignorance, illiteracy and superstition. We set out unmolested before it was generally known when we would be going, and I informed my fag husband that I would be returning in a few months. I had to make no big deal of it, as I said goodbye to my children with great difficulty. I had five extra camels packed into the caravan to spread out and lighten the load and speed the trip, but providence shone upon us and we went smoothly and safely and reached Muscat with no problems.

As the Prophet's daughter and sub-Iman's wife I was treated with great respect by the local head people. It was pretty disgusting in Muscat, but I knew I would not be there too long. After a short while, I chose four bodyguards to stay with us and sent the rest back to Medina. This was odd and would be questioned, but I had the reputation of doing odd things from time to time, and I would be long gone before anyone in Medina even knew that I had sent the bodyguards back.

A merchant boat carrying spices from the Malabar Coast of India had fortuitously arrived in Muscat after we had been there about eight days. Elijah went to talk to the captain about chartering the boat back to India. Confidential arrangements were quickly agreed to, and we loaded our stuff into the boat a few days later before dawn. We set sail to the port of Cochin just as a magnificent sunrise alit over the Arabian Sea. It was truly a new day dawning. The winds were quite favorable, and we landed in the ancient Jewish area of South India in the middle of the spice growing fertile storied land of the Coast of Malabar. It was as if I were escaping Hell and all the miserable citizens of Hell, striving to reach a neater, cleaner land, which was largely devoid of sand, morons, and camelshit. I was being reborn before my own eyes as a full adult; and I was as happy and expectant as I could be. Even as I was sailing into the ancient port of Cochin, I enjoyed the refreshing temperate breezes, saw the verdant, beautiful, lush hills and observed the rainbow that welcomed me at that magnificent moment. It reminded me of a thought I had not had for many years; my first friend and in many ways my true mother Ra'hel had always called me her rainbow child, for the first time, in this wonderful place; I felt that I fully understood her meaning. I was not made for a life surrounded by ugly, gritty, life-killing sand but for a more pleasant existence within an earthly paradise that had flowers, dark green lush trees and one, which produced a celebration of life with its multi-colored joyous rainbows.

CHAPTER FIFTY-THREE

Malabar

Even the name sounds exotic - Mal-a-bar. A beautiful place inhabited by friendly people with commerce and industry dynamically supporting a bountiful economy. The fecund region produced more spices than any other place on the earth, with heavily laden merchant boats full of ginger, black pepper, cinnamon, cardamom, fennel, cloves and other spices sailing out to a spice hungry world.

One of my first actions within this unspoiled tropical garden was hopefully my last despicable act. I had to protect my family, and that necessitated more evil from the woman who wanted so badly to do good. I was a little over halfway through pregnancy, and just beginning to show; with the first child that Elijah and I would have during this renaissance phase of our lives.

I wanted my old friends and assassins in Medina to think I was not only gone: but dead. The captain who took us to Cochin put me in touch with a boat going to Muscat, our guy vouched for this new captain as a clever and trustworthy soul. The second captain, who was paid well, spread a story in Muscat of the boat carrying the Prophet of Islam's daughter going down in a tempest close to the Indian shore with all hands and passengers lost, excepting one deck hand who survived. The story might not be believed and conflicting evidence might surface, but it would help freeze any action against me, I knew that as more time passed, the less I would be cared about. I was sure that the new Iman had plenty of other things to worry about, whether I was dead in Medina, dead in the Indian Ocean, or gone and very unlikely to ever come back, that it was all pretty much the same to him.

I threw a small party for Shahrazad and our servants to celebrate our safe arrival in the verdant paradisiacal land of coastal south India, and a different celebration for the four bodyguards. This affair was away from the ladies, inspired by the old parties we gave to our young men to show them the paradise reserved for soldiers who died battling for Allah. I had food, liquor and whores, and the young men we chose out of the twenty original bodyguards all liked booze and girls. At the hour of four A.M. Elijah checked in on the party. The girls had returned to their brothel and the men were drunk and deeply asleep. They were all stabbed to death and then quickly buried. They just knew too much and were the last link to our friends in Medina. I could no longer kill without regret, but the maternal instincts of an expectant mother demanded safety for her unborn child. They just had to go, and at least I gave them a to be dreamed of final night and a quick painless dispatch.

I asked, but did not demand, that all the servants, at least officially, convert to Judaism. They all decided to do so, which meant that all of us, me, Elijah, his children with Naomi, Shahrazad, and all the serving girls were now Jews. We moved into an estate outside of Cochin. Cochin was the only major Jewish settlement within all of India; and was encircled by a sea of Hindus. The 1000-year-old Jewish community was tolerated with no problems from its Hindu neighbors and lived in peace. Elijah and I had no problems fitting into the larger Jewish community. We bought a substantial working plantation and went into spice growing and trading.

I finally got a chance to make good on an old promise. Shahrazad at last found a fellow who was acceptable to both her and to me. She and I both knew that I was far wiser and had more experience with the male species than she could ever dream of having. She easily liked many men, but they generally were losers with a capital L. This was the one area in life where she had absolutely no smarts. Finally in Malabar, a more mature Shahrazad began eying a slightly younger man who came from an honest and hard working family that had not yet attained great financial success. He was a good looking, steady and pleasant man who appeared to have no bad habits. I gave Shahrazad a large dowry consisting of a moderately sized, and near by, working spice farm, valuable jewelry, and gold. She and Daniel wed, seemed to get along with few problems, and Shahrazad begat a son and daughter to her utter delight, as she continued as my best girlfriend and now social equal.

We would follow the events in Arabia, generally getting the news three to four months after the fact. I was certainly interested, but my life was now here in Malabar, and I was busy happily producing a child every fifteen to eighteen months.

I mellowed with age and enjoyed being a normal wife with a normal family without the intrigue and necessary duplicity of power and politics. We kept a relatively low profile and formed friendships with many similar Jewish families. I knew that as my second crop of children grew, they would be totally accepted into the highest levels of Cochin society, find spouses (or is that spice as in mouse-mice?) and good lives here within the pleasant, tropical Coast of Malabar.

My interest in all the Islamic camelshit and meshugas attenuated as the years slowly went by. An absolute evil presence had seized the movement; women were horribly repressed, and all the ancient Arabian stink of tribalism and just plain stupid meanness took over. The Koran kept on being severely amended to sanctify this evil anti-humanistic fanaticism. Islam was taking a harsh, take no prisoners, ugly tone, nurtured within the stifling hot, arid and foreboding peninsula that engendered it. I was so sickened and turned off by the new oppression and cruelty that had overwhelmed Islam. I might allow myself to curiously watch, but I wanted nothing to do with the religion.

Eventually Ali did live long enough and succeeded to become Iman or Caliph after the assassinations of the third and fourth Caliphs. It presented a golden opportunity for me to make a triumphant return to power, prestige and again become the embodiment of the apparition of Allah. There would be risk involved, and the usual crap, but obtainable. I just did not care, and who would want to leave this beautiful, lush, benign and happy place for the sands and camel stench of Arabia? I knew that someone was pulling Ali's strings, he could not even run a boys brothel right let alone a religious and political movement. I could not figure out who the puppet master was, but it really did not matter. I did not want the job.

I was extremely happy and contented, all of our children in both Arabia and Malabar were doing well with good prospects. Fuck Islam and the camel it rode in on. I am not saying that I was sorry that Old Mama gave her well-placed shove to the drunken Mohammad and started the whole process, but as far as I was concerned, it was over. Also, in the constant ironies that surround the beginning of the religion, the camel that Islam actually did ride in on, Old Mama, was actually fucked by Mohammad. She was publicly fucked many times, in many places, in front of many witnesses by the grand Prophet of Allah. I just wanted my true husband Elijah and myself and our children to live a normal good life away from all the insanity, perversion and drunken stupidity.

Besides, I figured, especially with the big crybaby, and laughingly still my legal husband, Ali, ostensibly running things, the whole circle of camelshit would quickly collapse, and the evil and misanthropic fanaticism which had taken over from me, would rapidly fade to obscurity, hopefully an altruistic and kind society, with a benevolent religion, would quickly replace it. In the history of the world, no person has ever been more wrong.